THE DEFENDERS

Ex-bounty hunter Jubal Thorne wants nothing more than to settle down to a peaceful life when he rides into Brewlins, Wyoming. What he gets is something else entirely. Caught up in a bidding wrangle for a local ranch with Abbey Watt, he buys the land and she buys the steers. But trouble is brewing with powerful cattleman Chas Stryker, who wants the spread for himself. When Thorne finds the former owner of his ranch shot dead in his own house, he knows he'll be defending his claim with his six-gun . . .

ALEX HAWKSVILLE

THE DEFENDERS

Complete and Unabridged

LINFORD
Leicester

First published in Great Britain in 2018 by
Robert Hale
an imprint of The Crowood Press
Wiltshire

First Linford Edition
published 2020
by arrangement with
The Crowood Press
Wiltshire

A catalogue record for this book is available
from the British Library.

ISBN 978–1–4448–4593–8

Published by
Ulverscroft Limited
Anstey, Leicestershire

Set by Words & Graphics Ltd.
Anstey, Leicestershire
Printed and bound in Great Britain by
TJ Books Limited, Padstow, Cornwall

This book is printed on acid-free paper

1

Jubal Thorne rode his horse, Ebony, along part of the Oregon Trail towards the town of Brewlins, Wyoming. He had been on the track for a long time now. There was something about the steady progress of horse and man through the long stretches of rolling country that calmed a mind that had once been fevered. Alone, without being lonely, he had time to dwell on thoughts of what had brought him to this point and why he had to keep riding onwards.

His journey had been made easier by the fact that the trail onto which he had moved was long established in this period of time, the eighties, so he was far from short of listeners. He would often come across herds being trailed across the wide sweep of the land, so he had spent many a night listening to tales of derring-do from cowboys hungry for fresh company while he was enjoying the warmth of their campfires. He had a story or two of his own to tell, and he was not averse to sharing the details with men who were often eager for novelty.

He was also able to bring news of what was happening in the towns and cities, and for men who were often separated from society for months at a time his presence was a welcome diversion. The long days riding the trail could be monotonous; especially when the landscape stretched towards the horizon as far as the eye could see. Rivers and trees broke it up now and then, but it was often rocky and dusty for what seemed like unending miles.

Life was not easy for him on the trail, however, despite his ability to take the endless days and the long nights alone with no one but his horse for company. Ebony was a large, quiet animal, robust and black as coal, with a touch of fiery temper and an intelligence that went far beyond the normal range for such animals. He was well able to carry his master and any baggage that Jubal might want to bring with him, but he was watchful and knowing, able to avoid trouble when it loomed before them, and easily able to outrun most of his kind.

Jubal was as fond of the animal as he was of anything — including other human beings — and he would often talk to the animal in a low, surprisingly cultured voice as they ambled along the trail. This was one of those occasions as they saw a welcome sign of civilisation. There was a huge uncultivated field covered in wild grass. Beside the field was a road that had been partially boarded to bear the weight of horses and carts in the winter, to the side of which was a plain wooden fence.

'Avery's,' said the sign painted on a board and stuck up at the side of the road. 'Trail eatery. Good fresh grub.'

'Well,' said Jubal, 'looks like we've landed all right.' Ebony twitched his ears and gave a faint whinny of agreement.

That was good enough for Jubal. He

dismounted from his steed. His wiry frame was aching from hours in the saddle as he led the animal forward towards a cluster of buildings from which the eatery stood out.

There was a stable at the side of the building, but this was obviously for the use of the ranchers only. In front of the eatery there was a trough full of fresh water and a bundle of hay. The owner of this place — the Avery mentioned on the sign — obviously knew that he had to cater a little for the animals of such visitors, and this was a good indication.

The eatery was a ranch-style building much like those lived in by those who had settled in this area, differing only in that it was slightly bigger than most. It was a long, low building with a shingled roof of dark, almost black tiles. There was a long porch out front supported at intervals by wooden pillars the thickness of a man's leg. These had been painted white to keep out dry rot. The porch was only one step high. The building had three different entrances; two for customers and, from the rich aroma drifting out from the third, he had a feeling this was where the kitchen would be. Out front of the building there was a wide expanse of grass on which grew large beech trees at regular intervals with jutting limbs. Altogether it was a good place to be. Jubal could feel his mouth watering as he stepped inside the building. It was midday and he had a feeling that he would have the place largely to himself. Inside he found what he had more or less expected, a few tables made of plain beech wood, about twenty robust chairs and a general feeling that here was a place that could be busy to the point of bursting. There was a menu hanging on the wall, which from the look of it was as unvarying as the wall itself, the lettering in capitals promising such delights as a fried platter, steak, sausages, and potatoes cooked in various ways, potato cakes, and a choice of tea, coffee and soft drinks.

There was a room off to one side where evidently some of the cowboys who frequented the eatery could go and relax a little, smoke, and play some barroom games.

The walls were plain and had been painted originally with whitewash that had darkened over the course of time to a kind of faded yellow, after cigarettes smoked by a thousand riders. Jubal felt at home, being a plain kind of man who had little time in his life for fripperies.

He took off his battered hat and laid it on the table, but he did not take off his long, black coat. He would do that when he was a little more relaxed, and he was well aware of the weight of the Peacemakers in his capacious pockets.

A large, cheerful-looking, overweight man of about fifty, who was well above middle height, bustled out of the kitchen. His striped shirtsleeves were rolled up and he wore a long white apron that fastened around his neck and his waist. His smile faded as he came towards Jubal.

'What do you want, mister?' He was eyeing the newcomer in a way that indicated he was not just asking what the traveller was going to eat. It was obvious straightaway that the man was thinking of telling him to leave. There was a shotgun leaning on the wall beside the kitchen door, which the newcomer noticed at the same time as the man appeared.

Somehow Jubal had strayed into hostile territory.

2

Whatever was going on, he decided to brazen it out for reasons of hunger alone.

'Guess I'll have the fried platter,' said Jubal, 'and a pot of coffee if you don't mind.' He was not the most sociable of men, but this newcomer might be his neighbour one day, so he got to his feet. 'The name's Thorne, Jubal Thorne.' He held out his hand, but the owner of the eatery did not respond in kind.

'The name's Merrill Avery,' he said. 'I'll get you your platter, Mr Thorne.' He started to walk away towards the kitchens at the foot of the building, weaving his way between the tables with unconscious ease. Just before going through the brown-framed doorway with the fringed curtain in place, he looked back. 'We don't want any trouble around here, mister.' He took the shotgun with him.

Thorne had already sensed an atmosphere about the place. There was a bleak feeling in the air that he had noticed as soon as the other man had appeared. Whatever was causing the feeling had nothing to do with business; the place was obviously thriving, so there had to be another reason why Avery was reacting as he did.

Could that reason be Thorne himself? He considered the matter carefully. He never made an attempt to conceal what he was, a fact that was a red rag to a bull for some people. With his long, thick coppery hair with streaks of grey, the strands that fell over one side of his face, his dark clothing and his long dusty coat, he looked precisely what he was: an adventurer who made a living by his own hand. He was aware that the dark green eye patch, visible when he spoke and his hair shifted, did not help matters either; nor did the glitter of certainty in his one visible eye. Everything about him spoke of the fact that this was not a man to be trifled with.

Avery came back with the mouth-watering platter of food and set it down. The plate held a good mixture: crispy bacon, two eggs, beans and blood pudding. The jug of coffee was large and the mug with it was easily twice the size of the average cup. The cowboys who came in here had big appetites and Avery did not scrimp on serving them the meals that they obviously demanded.

Thorne ate as much of the meal as he was able, which was about half, then paid attention to the coffee. He felt about as relaxed as he could, which was not hugely since he regarded any public place as potentially dangerous, but he was giving the impression of being relaxed and amiable.

'That sure was a good meal,' he said as Avery came forward and collected the remains. 'I'll certainly recommend your fine establishment. Just one more coffee then I'll be on my way.' This had

the desired effect and Avery even managed the faint semblance of a smile.
Thorne wondered what it was that could
have made such an amiable looking man
become so worried that the appearance
of a dark-clad drifter would set him on
edge.

There was a rattle as one of the doors
was flung aside and a woman entered
the eatery. Thorne, who was used to
sizing up people quickly, took her in
with a casual glance from his one good
eye.

The woman was above average height
compared with many of those he had
seen in the territory. She had a very
firm set of features, with sculpted
cheekbones and a full, generous mouth
with lips of the clichéd ruby red. When
she took off her wide-brimmed hat he
could see that her long black hair had
been tied back with a purple ribbon
into a long ponytail that hung down
her back. She looked to be in her late
twenties or early thirties. She wore a
dark blue shirt that failed to conceal a

generous figure. Her skirt was long; as was the fashion, it went almost down to the top of her dusty leather boots, but it was a plain garment as befitted a working woman. Thorne sensed that this was a woman who would give as well as she got, and for that reason alone he immediately found her interesting.

'Merrill,' she was saying, 'looks as if these beeves are good ones; we'll get 'em fattened up in no time.' She stopped speaking when she saw the newcomer still sitting there enjoying his coffee while Avery stood a little awkwardly beside him.

Although she had stopped speaking, Thorne knew that she was sizing him up in much the same way he had been doing with her when she had walked into the building.

She was seeing a man a little older than her with a partially concealed face, clad in dark clothes, with a lean body, and the look of someone who had killed many men in his time. She wouldn't be wrong to think this about him. He was no killer of innocents though, but then there was no way for her to know this.

'I saw your fancy horse outside,' she said. 'I guess I won't be talking about my business in front of you.'

'Beg pardon,' said Jubal, standing up, 'the name's Thorne, Jubal Thorne. I already know the name of this gentleman, so I'm just short of an introduction to your good self.'

'This is my . . . friend, Abbey Watt,' said Avery, completing the introductions. 'We're in business together, you might say.'

'Business seems mighty good,' said Jubal looking around the eatery.

'I guess you've finished your coffee,' said Abbey Watt. 'It's maybe time for you to move on.'

'Guess it is,' said Jubal. 'Got some business of my own in town.' He looked at them and gave a faint smile.

'Let's say it hasn't exactly been a pleasure meeting you.' She looked at him directly. 'So how are you connected with the CTA?'

'Abbey, I don't think this is the time,' interrupted Avery, who seemed to be the type of person who would rather swim with the tide than make waves.

'Just asking a civil question. Well?'

'You know, I just came here for some eats,' said Jubal, 'The letters CTA mean little or nothing to me.'

'Then you'd better learn them pretty fast, Mr Thorne, because that's what you're up against around here.'

'It's the Cattle Trading Association,' said Avery with an apologetic air. 'Never had much truck with them myself, not after the early days when I was a cattle rancher before I had the bright idea of opening this place.'

'Seems as if you have a good set-up here,' said Thorne, 'but it's none of my business. Just one thing though, a question for you both; is there any land around here a man can acquire, say a smallholding that's already in force?'

'What do you mean by that?' asked Abbey Watt. 'What are you getting at?' It was obvious that there was an undercurrent of anger here that had nothing to do with the newcomer, but that was being fuelled by his appearance. One of the reasons Thorne was still alive for so long after taking up his business of bounty hunter — the very one he was trying to renounce — was that he knew when to make a strategic withdrawal.

'So, I suppose the name of Chas Stryker means nothing to you?' asked Abbey Watt in that strangely disconcerting and forthright manner of hers.

'Guess it's time to go, let you two get on with your business,' Thorne looked around the eatery again. 'You run a tight ship here, Mr Avery; it's been a pleasure meeting you. You too, ma'am, and I hope we can have a more civilised conversation one day.' He put on his hat and went outside to where the big stallion was waiting patiently for his master. Thorne untied the reins from the hitching post and mounted his steed.

He should have been feeling content

after his good meal and the hour or so off the trail, but he was feeling more than a little baffled by the exchange with Avery and his companion.

As he rode towards Brewlins the thought entered his head that perhaps he was entering into a world in which he would have to watch his back. But then again, that was precisely what he had been doing for years, so the thought did not bother him too much. He was prepared for trouble and, as long as he didn't cause any, he would take whatever the world threw at him.

3

The eatery was in a good position, stationed as it was at the head of Clearwater Valley. This was a route that had been opened in the days of Lewis and Clark when they were mapping the lands of the west. The great explorers had found the valley to be the perfect place for them to hunt game and feed their horses because of the rich grasses that grew in the region where the river was broadened by snow melts from the surrounding hills. Thorne, who had done his homework before coming to the area, knew it was also a place that was attractive to settlers after the new Homesteading Act had come into force. It looked to him as if Abbey Watt was one of those settlers, albeit one who had been there for a while in a different capacity. He could not get the expression on her face out of his mind. Here was a good-looking forthright woman, who underneath all the anger and bluster was just plain scared.

As he mulled over these thoughts he heard the rumble of hoofs and saw four mustangs coming along the main road pulling a large buckboard, raising a cloud of dust in the process. The buckboard was being driven by a thickset man with a facial fungus that bristled as he urged the horses on. Two other men steadied themselves in the back, holding onto piles of basic wood and wire fencing, the kind of which was used to enclose some of the green pastures about which Thorne had been thinking. He wondered where they had come from, but where they were going was not a mystery. They headed down past the eatery, the rumbling of the horses' hoofs and the clattering of the wooden wheels soon receding into the distance.

The purposeful movement of the vehicle, and the way it was loaded high, spoke volumes to Thorne. These were not only men who knew what they were doing and where they were going; they had done this before and knew exactly what they were up to.

The road lifted up on the way into Brewlins so Thorne was unable to get a good view until he was almost there. His first impression was that this was a tight little town built around the usual features of a main street, stores, church and livery, all-important features out here where a sense of community was created by common purpose. The Carbon hills loomed in the background, making the town look smaller than it was. The streets were wide and several trails led not just into the town but around it too. His expert eye immediately picked up the fact that these were where the big ranchers beyond the town would bring their cattle through. It also explained why the town was thriving, because a place where riders needed to lead beeves along, and horses could be tethered, would always be prosperous the way things were for now.

Thorne rode into town and hitched

his steed outside the Wooden Barrel saloon. He entered through the batwing doors and found the place was mostly empty.

'Dabs, you can't go around saying those things,' protested a man at the bar, who stood with a striking individual who wore an unmistakeable air of authority.

'You think?' countered this individual. 'This ain't the beer talking. Sure as my name is Dabney Wingate, I tell you she's going to ruin it for us.'

Thorne barely glanced at the two men as he went up to the bar and ordered a beer of his own from a large, indifferent barman, who seemed to be keeping a close eye on the two men. They barely glanced at the newcomer, since he was just another trail rider, many of whom would pass through on their way to the south. Thorne, however, was listening closely since his future had often depended on keeping his mouth shut and paying attention. There could only be one woman who was causing this kind of trouble. His theory was confirmed a few minutes later when the man called Wingate sneered again and wiped some suds off his thin mouth.

'See, Jim, this Abbey Watt's no more than a common slut who's got too big for her boots. She was working her way over that Brewlins hotel when she got lucky — or so she thought.' He glowered and took another draught of his beer.

'She fell in with Avery,' said the individual called Jim, not looking too happy about having it dragged out of him.

'See, if she'd stayed where she belonged, there wouldn't be this trouble,' said Wingate, 'but she's just a whore who's way too uppity for a dame.'

This seemed to be too much for the barman. He was bigger than both his customers. He wiped his hands on a cloth and made signs of coming out from behind the bar. He looked as if he had thrown a few men through the batwing doors out into the dirt road in his time.

'You gents better get a civil tongue in your head when you talk about a woman, any woman, or you're out of here fast.' The barman put his hands together and cracked his knuckles.

'All right, we're just leaving,' said Wingate. 'Drain your beer, Lewis. We don't have to put up with no bar hopper interfering with our private conversations.'

'I ain't hurrying,' said Lewis, 'and I've a fire-iron at my side that says I can stay.'

'All right,' said the barman, 'but you two watch your tongue. Abbey Watt is well thought of around here.'

He returned to his duties behind the bar, while the two men continued talking in low voices. Thorne struggled to hear what was being said, but pretended indifference as he listened on.

'Don't matter what anyone says,' muttered Jim Lewis. 'Sutter, Venters and Big Mac are makin' sure that lady is going to get her comeuppance.'

'Should've stayed like it was,' said

22

Wingate, brooding. 'This Homesteading Act's been the problem, taking away the access we've been used to, giving her a chance to get 160 acres she don't deserve through her lies. Well, we'll hear their progress when they comes back.'

Thorne knew that they were just going to leave, so he turned and put out a hand to the barman.

'Name's Thorne,' he said, 'what's yours?'

'They call me Starry,' said the barman. 'How can I help you, mister?'

'Well, Starry, you seem to know the lie of the land around here. I'm looking for some information that'll help me get a toe into local business.'

'Sure, anything that brings in business is good,' said the barman. 'More customers for me since I own this here establishment.'

'See, I was going to go to a land agent, but in the past they seemed a bit too intent on lining their own pockets at my expense,' said Thorne, 'so here's a direct question: is there a ranch in this region up for sale? I have the funds to buy direct.'

'Sure, there's a place out in the Coltsfoot Hills,' said Starry, 'owned by Old Tom Bate. He's looking for a buyer. He'll be available if you want to see him and talk terms.'

'Think you can write down a few directions for me?'

'Sure,' said the bar owner. He went to the back to fetch a piece of paper and scribbled down a few directions. While he was doing so, Thorne became aware that he was now an object of attention for the two men who had been discussing Abbey Watt. The looks they were giving him were openly hostile and he wondered what festering sore he had opened now. It seemed that the two men were steeped in some kind of resentment. Thorne pretended that he could not see their hostile glances as the barman came back with the scribbled instructions.

'See, you just go out of this side of town, right across the herd trail and through a wide pass, you'll find Tom's holding out there,' said Starry helpfully. 'Reckon he'll be eager to take you up on your offer if it's just right.'

'Why is he selling up?'

The barman shrugged. 'I guess times change and he doesn't have any family here now. Most of his stock is gone, his health ain't too good, and a lot of his hands have been poached by Stryker.'

'*Mister* Stryker, to you,' interrupted Wingate.

'You boys still here? Thought you was heading.'

'Come on Jim, some of us have real work to do.' Wingate strolled out followed by his stolid companion.

'Stryker's men?' asked Thorne.

'Avoid them, they're trouble,' said Starry.

Thorne intended to do just that. He thanked the barman and strode out of the saloon to fetch his horse. No time like the present and he knew where to go now. Then he heard a grating voice from behind.

'Stop right where you are, mister.'

4

Thorne felt a tingling between his shoulder blades that told him there was real trouble heading his way. He turned slowly just to show that he was in charge of his own movements, and found that he was looking at Wingate and his companion who, contrary to their avowal of going back to work, had clearly been waiting for him to come out of the somewhat rough-and-ready establishment he had been gracing with his presence.

'So, gentlemen, how can I help you?'

'Who are you, *Thorne*?' asked Wingate in much the same tones that he had used when describing Abbey Walt.

'Reckon that's my business,' said Thorne evenly. 'Jubal Thorne's the name.' He had never conducted much of his business in Wyoming. Most of the felons he had hunted down had been in Arizona and New Mexico, so he did not expect his name to have much resonance around these parts, but Wingate was giving a frown of recognition as the name stirred some faint memories. Of course these were cattle traders, used to being on the trail, and stories were swapped around in such circumstances. The reason he had come here was to forget his past, but it looked as if it was not going to be forgotten so easily by those he encountered.

'The name's familiar,' said Wingate. 'I'll make the connection, but leaving that aside, I want to know why you're interested in Old Tom's place.'

'Never heard of the place,' said Thorne, 'but it sounds like an interesting proposition.'

'You hear that Jim, this here new arrival Mr Thorne thinks Old Tom's place sounds like an interesting proposition.'

'Sure, I can understand that,' said Lewis. 'Place like that's got possibilities, if you want to stay dirt poor that is.'

'I don't understand what you're getting at,' said Thorne. He was standing in the street now. The weather had been dry for some time and the soil beneath his feet was solid, compacted by the pounding of thousands of hoofs. As he spoke to them he gradually moved around so that the sun was no longer glinting into his eyes over Wingate's right shoulder. He was aware of the comforting weight of the Peacemakers in his capacious pockets. These men, whoever they were, did not really know him. He supposed that this knowledge and his unnatural calmness were a factor in their behaviour, for they were both armed. He noted that Wingate's hand hovered over the well-worn butt of his Colt .45, while Lewis had pulled back his waistcoat to reveal his own weapon. 'So, what do you mean by 'stay dirt poor'?'

'See, the cattle business is changing,' said Wingate, 'ain't that right, Jim?'

'You never said a truer word, boss.'

'For the record, Thorne, there's a move towards consolidating business around these here parts if you know what I mean.'

'Stock growers and breeders,' said Thorne agreeably. 'I've heard word.'

'Then you'll have heard of the Cattle Trading Association,' said Wingate. 'Around here we got five main big ranchers. They handle hundreds of thousands of steers a year between them, and my boss, Charles Stryker, just happens to be the head of that very Association. They all pay a fee to join and they all look after each other's interests.'

'Still don't see what this has to do with me,' said Thorne.

'Well, what are your plans?'

'You know, a man has a right to keep his secrets,' said Thorne, keeping his voice as agreeable as possible. 'Truth is, I don't know what my plans are, I'm just interested in what you said about staying dirt poor.' He nodded to Lewis.

'See, it's a numbers game,' said Lewis. 'You got a few head of cattle. You don't make much profit on that herd, but you still got to feed 'em and breed 'em, so what happens is that in bad times you still got all the overheads but none of the profit. Now with the Cattle Trading Association, the big five can share all their resources, ain't that right, Win?'

'Sure is,' said Wingate, 'it means that instead of having to fight each other we can share common land. Hell, in the busy season, the big cattle drives, we can even share men just to get the herding done and the beeves on their way.'

'Doesn't sound so good for the little man,' said Thorne. 'Looks as if you would just bully him out of the way and take what you wanted. Looks as if that way of working ain't exactly fair.'

'So that's why buying a place like Old Tom's would be a great recipe for starting poor and stayin' poor,' said Wingate in a would-be reasonable voice. 'You got money to invest? You could do worse than open another saloon right here in Brewlins,' he added, 'you'd make a fine

30

barkeep with that lean look and strange mop of yourn.'

'Well, gents, only time will tell,' said Thorne. He nodded to them and turned to go away.

'Wait, so where are you headed?' grated Wingate.

Thorne knew that this was the time for him to tell a lie, to keep the peace, but there was a part of him that did not submit to this kind of force. Again he felt that tingling in his spine as he turned, hands ready at his pockets, the reassuring weight of his guns at his upper thighs.

'Going for a ride in the hills like a free citizen,' he said.

'Going to the Bates place after all?'

'I'll see where the ride takes me.' This was when their fate was being decided, although neither of them knew it. Thorne was aware that there was a bead of sweat on Wingate's face. The trail boss stared hard at the lone traveller and once more his right hand hovered over his weapon. But it was a busy day, lots of passers-by on the boardwalks, and

Thorne seemed to be unarmed. Wingate was not a stupid man.

'We'll speak again,' he said. 'Come on, Jim,' and the pair turned away.

★ ★ ★

Abbey Watt was facing Merril Avery and the look on her face was one of sheer determination. Avery was shifting uncomfortably; this was a woman whom he had known for years but he was still mesmerised by her force of personality. He was no slouch in that area himself; having seen what was happening to the smaller cattlemen, he decided instead to concentrate on opening his range store and eatery. Now he was wilting under her glare.

'You know what they're doing now, Merrill? They're fencing in the land down at the Narrows.'

'Ain't nothing we can do to stop them,' he said, aware that his words seemed feeble even to himself. 'We ain't got the manpower. I've got the girls who work here and a couple of older hands who mow the hay and keep the place stocked, you've only got the two boys.'

'They're not boys,' she said briskly, 'they're young men as far as I'm concerned and they're big and strong. They could be a mighty help with what I want.'

'And what do you want?'

'I want to do some de-fencing, Merrill.' He gave a groan at this and threw his hands in the air. Being a short-order cook and having to be sensitive to issues had made him more expressive than the usual range dweller.

'Listen to yourself. You know there's more than Big Stryker involved in this: there's Snow, Gracie, Williams and Parmiter and the other traders. It just happens to be Stryker's men down there because they're the closest and he's the biggest.'

'But they're starting to encroach on my claim. I've been there the two years required. My claim is legitimate now.'

33

She lowered her voice and suddenly some of the old Abbey came through. '*Our* claim.'

'Don't talk like that,' he said looking around nervously, even though there was no one else around. They both shared the knowledge that under the Homesteading Act, the settlers could hold no more than 160 acres each. He already had his own land, and it was well established. When Abbey had come to work for him, with her determination to make her way in the world, it had seemed like manna from heaven. He would be able to expand, finally charge for the use of the meadows, and do it through this more-than-willing woman. The trouble was that, right now, he was feeling like Pandora who had let out a lot more from the box than was safe.

'What do you aim to do?' he asked, aware even as he said the words that they sounded feeble even to his own ears.

'First thing I'm going to do is go into town and hire me a few more hands, out of my own savings, to undo what they've been doing,' she said briskly. 'We have a lot of friends in Brewlins.'

'Not as many as will stand up against the CTA,' he said.

'You could be right, but there's another thing you haven't addressed.' This time he gave an audible groan. 'I'm talking about that lone gunman.'

'I knew you were going to say something about him.'

'I'm going to give him a hard time, again through my friends. I'll make sure he knows he isn't wanted around here.'

'He could've just been a legitimate traveller.'

'What, just when they're encroaching on my land? Just when they're bounding off the good feed to shut me off from my own meadows?' He had to admit there was a lot of sense in her words; it did seem an odd coincidence.

'Mind you,' said Merrill, 'these things have a way of happening. He could be just another settler.' He let his shoulders droop in a way that showed he was resigned to what she was about to do. 'All right, we ain't busy until later. I'll get some of the girls to fill in if there happens to be any trade.' He started to take off his apron.

'What are you doing?' she asked.

'Coming with you.'

'I don't think I made myself clear enough. I'm going into town on my own.'

'But what about Stryker's men?'

'What about 'em? That bunch of cattle prodders are busy fencing, most of 'em anyway, an' I've got this.' She pulled aside her dark yellow jacket and showed him the shiny new Colt at her waist. 'You got to deal with these things right away, if'n they want to try me I'll try them right back.' He shook his head as she left, knowing that she would never let him go with her. He tidied up the serving area, sweeping away the remnants of the stranger's meal. He went through the kitchen area, and from long experience partly cooked up some meat for the evening trade. It was midweek so he wouldn't be hugely busy. He knew his business.

In the meantime Abbey Watt rode into town, her broad-brimmed hat protecting her head from the afternoon sun. Her experienced eye took in the trail left by Jubal Thorne less than an hour before. Once in town she hitched her dappled mare outside the Brewlins Hotel, a familiar and well-frequented landmark, and headed for the Wooden Barrel saloon, the first port of call for anyone coming to town. As she rounded the corner, and was in the shadow of the boardwalk on Fuller Street, she could see three men. Two of them were standing far enough away from the third to show this was no mere chat. There was real resentment in the air; she could feel it even from that distance. There, in the shadows, she was able to hear exactly what was being said. As she withdrew back around the corner and waited for the men to depart, there was a thoughtful look on her face.

5

Thorne was making his way around the corner, looking for somewhere to stay. He missed very little and saw Abbey Watt going into the Wooden Barrel saloon. He wondered how much she had heard of his little exchange with the ranchers. He immediately saw the sign for the Brewlins Hotel. Trees were a precious resource in this stony landscape, and the hotel had been built in the pioneering days to house those adventurers who were establishing coal mines in the area, and then added to later for those engaged in commissioning and overseeing the building of the railroads.

Because of the lack of wood the building had been made of the same local yellow stone as the facade of the state penitentiary on the extreme edge of town. They called the stone yellow, but it had deeper hues of orange and red within and was not a displeasing colour. The structure was three storeys high and looked as if it had plenty of room in its deeper recesses. The windows were a little too small for his taste, with no wooden balconies on the outer edge. In other words it was a place where a man could be holed up if he wasn't too careful.

And Thorne was always careful.

Two men appeared in front of him as he led Ebony across to the hotel.

They were dressed in a similar fashion, with blue shirts, sleeveless waistcoats and dark trousers. They both wore long leather boots and walked in a way that showed they were habitual users of horses, spurs jangling as they did so. Both wore wide-brimmed hats to keep off the sun. They could have been brothers, but one was much younger than the other. Only the stars pinned to the left of either waistcoat, along with the way they stood in front of the man and his steed as if they had right of way, showed that they had the power of the law behind them.

'Name's Matt Buck,' said the older of the two with an easy assurance. 'Beggin' to introduce myself, and my colleague here: Bud, Bud Atkins. Might a man enquire who he's speaking to?'

'He might,' said Thorne, without offering any more information. In his experience there were two kinds of lawmen: those who were under the control of the big businesses of the area, and those who would actually do their jobs more or less impartially. He was trying to draw the man out with his indifference.

'See, we've heard there's a bit of trouble down the valley,' said Matt Buck. 'Ain't that right, Bud?'

'It sure is, Sheriff,' agreed his deputy.

'Now, when we see someone like you coming to town, we get to wondering who you are and where you've been and what you're up to.'

'Got a little money to invest, just making my way,' said Jubal.

40

'Still didn't get the name.'

'Well, I've got to get on with my day, gentlemen. I've had a long ride to get here, I want to get settled and then get on with some business.'

Thorne was weakening; he knew that he could give them his name and just get on with his day. He was about to do this, moving his head as he did so, and the copper-coloured hair that concealed the left side of his face fell aside and revealed his dark green eye patch and a little of the outline of his face.

'Wait,' said Bud Atkins. 'That eye patch, that there face. Matt, I think I know who this is.'

'Guess I already know,' said the sheriff. 'You're Jubal Thorne, ain't you?'

'I didn't know my fame had spread so widely,' said Thorne, trying to keep it light.

'We hear stories in the law business,' said Buck. 'Besides, Bud here, he started out in the rail business, decided he wanted a little more to his life and applied to be my deputy. He's been around, heard the stories.' The lawman was taller than Thorne by quite a few inches. He drew himself up to his full height and puffed out his chest. 'From what I've heard you've killed quite a few men, Thorne.'

Jubal neither confirmed nor denied this.

'Don't know who's hired you or why they brought you here,' added Buck,' but I'm guessing that sooner or later you're going to be involved with Stryker and the Cattlemen's Trading Association. Just a warning to you, if either of us hears that you've been brought in to sort out that little problem in the valley, you is going to be mighty sorry.'

'I suppose this Stryker needs some help from law,' said Thorne indifferently. He actually saw the sheriff swell up with anger.

'Now, you see here, I uphold the law because that's my duty. Mr Stryker, he's a big bug around here, but if he does any wrong, he gets the same treatment as everyone else.'

'Matt don't like the CTA much,' added Bud.

'Shut your fool mouth,' said the sheriff. 'Well, whose side are you on, Mr Thorne?'

'That's easy,' said Thorne, 'my own. I came here to make a new start. Believe me, my past is gone.'

'It better be,' said the sheriff. 'You stick out like the sorest of thumbs around here, and we want this place to settle down, not grow worse. No doubt we'll meet again.' Both he and the deputy nodded to the new arrival and made their way down Fuller Street, while Jubal continued to the hotel, hitching Ebony to the post outside.

He had a lot of food for thought as he made his way into the building. There was an older man behind the desk of the hotel. Thorne could see at once that both the hotel and the man had seen better days; there was an air of faint neglect about the place. He booked three nights in the hotel and was given a room on the first floor. The ground floor area had been given over to the front room where residents could sit, a bar, and a place where people could dine that was not exactly a restaurant but had another bar. He had the impression that business was not brisk, but then it was just after winter and many of the trails had yet to begin.

Having satisfied himself that the accommodation was in order, he brought up his worldly goods — which were not great in number because he had learned how to travel light — deposited them on the iron-framed bed and went back out to the big stallion. Thorne was still wrestling with what he had learned about the place.

'Don't worry,' he told his horse, 'this'll be the last ride of the day, Eb boy.' The horse twitched his ears back and gave a snort of derision at this, but he still had plenty of go in him and he wasn't about to let Thorne down. The latter was just about to get into the big Western saddle when a figure in a dark, flowing skirt came trotting rapidly towards him and he recognized the big, good-looking woman from earlier. He tipped his hat to her.

'Mr Thorne, don't go yet.'

'Sorry, ma'am, I have a bit of business to conduct and it's been a long day.'

'This won't take long.'

'How can I help you?'

'I heard your little exchange with Wingate earlier on. It seems you were telling the truth.' She had been looking at him with big, blue, questioning eyes; now she had the grace to lower her gaze. 'I'm sorry, Mr Thorne, I jumped to conclusions because of the way you looked. It's just that they're starting to make it plain that I'm getting in their way.'

'Who are 'they'?'

'The Cattleman's Trading Association. They've united together in such a way that if anyone gets in their way that person gets stamped on hard.'

'That's not uncommon; it's the way with all businesses, Mrs Watt.'

'Call me Abbey, and I'm no-one's 'Mrs', if you want to know.'

'Begging pardon, ma'am, but you're a fine looking woman; I'm surprised you haven't been snapped up.' He could see immediately that this line of talk was not something she was going to allow to continue.

'What I have to do with men or anyone else is my business, Mr Thorne. The thing is, I've been hearing a lot about you, that you have a certain reputation.'

'I am not about to confirm or deny anything,' he said. 'I'm not about reputation, I just want to make a new start and it's the way of this land. I've made some money and I intend to settle down with a place of my own.'

'Leaving that aside, don't you have a need for justice?'

The question was one he considered for a few seconds. 'I've had a long day; guess I'll just go about my business and see you around, Miss Watt.'

'Look, it's as simple as this, I know

who you are and what you are,' said Abbey Watt, the colour rising in her cheeks. 'I think I'm making myself plain.'

'Could be.'

'I can give you a green backing, and an introduction to people in town. Life can get a lot easier if you help me.'

He looked at her thoughtfully and shook his head.

'Can't see that it's possible, ma'am, not the way things stand.'

Her face was flooded crimson now, but with anger rather than shame. 'You're just like the rest; it doesn't bother you when it doesn't affect you. Well, if you don't help me, further along the line they'll come to get you. That's the truth, plain and simple.'

'Thanks for the warning. I guess we'll be neighbours in a manner of speaking but right now I've got a trip to take.'

'Where are you going?'

'Just to see a man called Tom Bate. They say he can put a little transaction my way. Sounds good to me.' He tipped

47

his hat to her, and she turned away with a stony look on her face: the look of an individual who had suddenly made a grim decision.

48

6

He rode Ebony out of town, the hoofs of the big animal kicking up clouds of dust as they headed out towards Coltsfoot Pass. The lie of the land was rugged, and the landscape was fairly bare except for scrubby grass and low-lying yellow sage as he headed towards the minor valley behind that very pass.

His mind was absorbed by getting to where he was going, particularly now that time was passing. The sooner he could make some sort of trade with the Old Man, the sooner he could have a place of his own and get out of town. Then he could start hiring a few hands and get to work on his plans. He became aware that there was a pounding of hoofs behind him as he came to the flatter land, and he looked around. Abbey Watt was riding her grey mare, long hair streaming out behind her as she rode, and she was catching up with him fast. Even as he saw the gun in her hand, the weapon went off just as he was reaching the echoing, jagged walls of the pass and the sound reverberated off the walls. Startled by the shot that passed close to his head, Ebony reared and bucked, throwing his master to the ground.

Fortunately Thorne was the kind of person who was prepared. He had shallow stirrups, pulled his feet out as soon as he knew he was going to be thrown, and landed on the ground, on his feet, like a cat.

The woman's horse was coming towards him, so without a second's thought he reached out, grabbed her flowing skirt and her waist and gave a heave. He was much stronger than he looked, having the stringy kind of body that is like steel wire, and she flew from her saddle as he allowed her own weight to carry her to the ground, only supporting her to prevent her from crashing to the rocky soil and being injured.

He pulled her to her feet, holding her by the wrists, and the pistol that she had somehow retained slipped from her fingers and rattled against the ground.

'What do you mean by it?' he grated. The movements made had shifted aside his coppery locks and she was looking into the face of a demon, a demon with one glittering eye. The sight was unnerving and she was startled enough to speak.

'I'm sorry; I didn't want to hurt you. I just wanted to stop you from getting what I need. The brand, I can't lose the brand.' He helped her to her feet and she rapidly dusted down her dress. He did not try to help her; oddly enough, laying hands on her now would be considered a measure of impropriety.

Before he could continue questioning her there was sound of clattering hoofs. They were at the wide entrance to the pass and a huge roan heaved into view carrying a big man in his late fifties wearing a sheepskin jacket and a buff-coloured hat, with a pair of old shooting irons at his sides. Instinctively Thorne knew who the stranger was from that unmistakeable air of arrogance the man exuded without trying. For this reason too he stepped back, pulling his heavy hair into place in one instinctive motion, hiding the true nature of his features.

'How do, Miss Watt?' said the rider.

'Good afternoon, Mr Stryker,' said Abbey Watt, straightening her back and looking defiantly up at his big face.

'Call me Chas,' said the newcomer. From the look on her face it was clear that this was one instruction she was going to ignore. 'So who's this with you?'

'Just a friend,' said Jubal Thorne. 'Thorne's the name. Miss Watt here, she's taking the time to show me around.'

'Well don't go near that cuss down there,' said Stryker. 'Stubborn old fool. Doesn't know a good deal when he hears it. I offered a deal for his brand and his cattle, but no go on that one.'

'I have a question for you, about my land,' said Abbey Watt. 'Why the fencing?'

'Ain't no law against a small claim being made,' said Stryker. 'Wingate's mighty fond of that part of the valley, pushing out on his own.'

'You liar! You're doing all the fencing in, stealing the meadows that could be used with my claim,' said Abbey. 'Just get the hell out, Mr Stryker.'

'Don't know what you're talking about and don't have the time,' said Stryker. 'Well, good to meet you, Mr Thorne. Guess I'll be on my way. See you, Miss Abbey.'

'Go to hell,' she said. Stryker chuckled out loud this time, cracked his reins and the big horse trotted away until both man and animal were lost to sight. The other two did not move until he was no longer visible against the undulating hills outside town.

'What do you say we call a truce for just now?' asked Thorne. 'Looks to me as if we both have an aim in mind, and there's no reason why we can't see this Tom fella together.'

'You would forgive me taking a pot in your direction?'

'Guess I wouldn't. You give me that gun and you ride in front where I can keep an eye on you.'

'What if I say no?'

'I have some spare traces, I can tie you up and throw you over your horse if you want, and we'll get there either way.' He tucked her gun into his belt and they mounted their respective steeds, riding into the valley like an old married couple, with the woman just slightly ahead.

The ranch turned out to be a collection of mostly rundown feed sheds, a barn, and a ranch house that was in need of some repair. There was a corral to one side with a couple of indifferent roans in it, and a worn pasture with some low fencing that held a couple of dozen cattle.

As they got off their horses, a figure came running stiffly out of the ranch and down the three sagging steps that led down from the porch. The whiskery old man was hatless, dressed in brown overalls, and held a double-barrelled shotgun. He spoke in breathless tones.

'Git out of here, I don't do no truck with you, I told you.' Then he stopped short and gazed at the new arrivals.

'Why, it's Miss Abbey, but who's this with you? Is this a trick of that bastard?'

'Tom, we're both here about something you have to sell,' said Abbey. The old man came up close to Thorne and squinted into the latter's face, his breath redolent of whiskey, and not the expensive kind either.

'This is a mighty strange arrival,' said he. 'All right, come in and let's talk.' He did not, however, turn his back and lead the way. Instead he let them go forward while he still clutched at his shotgun, watching them closely as they went inside the ranch.

They were hit by a scent that was a mixture of old-man reek and cat. The furnishings were sparse and they sat in wooden chairs while the old man settled down gingerly in a rocking chair with a padded seat.

'Don't pay him any heed, Tom,' said Abbey immediately, 'I'm here to buy your remaining stock for a fair price. But most of all, I want your brand. There, I've kept it simple for you.'

'If I wanted the brand and the beasts,' asked Thorne, 'would you sell them to me if I outbid this lady?' He had already introduced himself by then.

'Well, mister, you ain't from around these parts. Don't see why I should trust you; for all I know you could be an agent of the CTA, taking it all for Charles Stryker.' The old man gave a sudden, unexpected laugh. 'I showed him already with old Bessie here.' He stroked the shotgun, which he had left at his side, almost fondly. 'So I reckon I'll listen to the lady first.'

'Why don't you just buy a brand?' asked Thorne of the woman, 'instead of taking the trouble to shoot at free citizens?'

'Because the CTA control everything around here,' she said in that fierce manner of hers. 'They've priced it so high, thousands of dollars for a brand that us small people can't afford. The only way to get a reasonably priced brand is to join the CTA, and you can't join unless you have thousands of cattle. Oh, it's a nice little cartel.'

'Seems you could make a tidy profit,' said Thorne, 'begging your pardon, Tom, but I could easily outbid her.'

'The woman gets the brand, the Lazy B iron, and at a fair price,' said the old man.

'Then I guess there's no more to be said about that,' said Thorne, while the woman looked visibly relieved. 'In truth, I don't care about your brand, I'm here for an altogether different reason.' He was aware that Abbey was looking at him with a mixture of relief and annoyance. She obviously still had a distrust of his intentions, and he could not blame her altogether in this. However, Thorne had been playing a little game of his own, keeping his reasons obscured until the facts of the situation were more plainly out in the open. It was a ploy he had often used in the past when conducting his business. 'I want to buy the freehold off you, lock, stock and barrel.'

'Well, you've put yourself in a mighty pickle,' said the old man, ' 'cause I've just told you both the brand's going. The cattle too, if I've a mind.'

'It's not that kind of business I want this place for,' said Thorne. 'You have some grazing land and plenty of space for an extra corral. From what I've seen, the cattle business is a little bit too contentious for me; I'll hire some local hands and do some horse-breeding up here.'

'Then there's two negotiations,' said Bate. 'I'll need to speak to Miss Watt alone. You can take a walk, mister. I'll shout you later.' Again he stroked his shotgun with abnormal fondness. Jubal was good at taking a hint and stepped out of the building with great dignity. He walked around the ranch, taking in the lie of the land and the buildings with an expert eye. The ranch was in not too bad condition considering there had been few repairs done in the last few years. All in all, there would need to be a degree of investment, but he was serious with regard to this. Up here in the hills he would be as far away from his past as he had ever been, and as time went on his reputation for horse breeding would grow and his past would fade. At last he heard a shout and Abbey Watt appeared. 'He'll see you now,' she said, looking happy with regard to her own situation.

'Did you get the brand?'

'Yes, as a matter of fact; what's it to you, mister?'

'There you go again, letting loose that suspicious tongue of yours.' She had the grace to look ashamed.

'I'm sorry; when you've been backed into a corner a few times you get into the habit of lashing out. I'd best get back to town.'

'Wait for me. I happen to think

59

there's power in numbers and you don't know if Stryker's still around.'

'Why, Mr Thorne, I do believe you're trying to be a gentleman. I may wait.' She went down the steps; he went past her and into the gloom of the building. The old man was sitting there looking genial but suspicious.

'Well, tell me why I should let you have the Bate spread?'

'Why are you selling up, if you don't mind me asking?'

'Well, my good wife, she went a few years ago, died of the fever,' said Bate. 'My boys went out east, and I let them go. They were bright lads. Now they both have lives in New York. I had a few good hands working for me at the time, but they're all gone now: dead, retired, or poached by the CTA.'

'And what are you going to do?'

'I've had an offer. My eldest boy'll have me: I won't be a burden to anyone, and I'll pay my own way and join him and his family. A man gets weary trying to keep the place going, especially in the winter. It can be mighty cold up here, with snow blowing in, so it's time to get out while there's a chance.' He fixed Thorne with glittering eyes from beneath his shaggy brows. 'Brewlins ain't what it was; uster be just a pioneer town, but now there's bullies and murderers around and all in the name of big profit. You are wise to keep out of the cattle game if that's your intention.'

'It sure is, to breed horses and lead a quiet life.'

The old man looked at him sharply. 'You might want to lead a quiet life, but will life leave you alone?'

It was an unanswerable question.

7

Thorne returned to the Brewlins hotel, but only after riding down the trail that led to Clearwater Valley along with Abbey Watt. On the way there he told her about the men he had seen earlier on, but she did not seem the least surprised. He could see from the tightening of her jaw and the look on her face that this was not something she was going to take lying down. Part of him wanted to offer his help, but he knew better than to interfere in an affair that had nothing to do with him. Still, he gave her back her pistol and parted from her with a sense of regret. He liked her determination, but they were going to meet again soon. Thorne, who was no slouch in that area of business, was going to arrange for the three of them — including the old man — to go and see a lawyer on the morrow.

Where there is business there will be lawyers. Once more Thorne relied on his own instincts and looked around the centre of town until he found a shingle beside a modest, respectable-looking office. 'Justin Bowers,' he said aloud. The name had a satisfying ring to it. This done, he returned to his hotel. It had been one of the longest days of his life. He made sure that Eb was bedded down, and headed back into the building for a drink and a smoke before bed. He went out like an extinguished candle, the grim thoughts in his head far from enough to keep awake his exhausted body.

The next day, as good as his word, he fetched Eb from the livery, but only after speaking to Justin Bowers, a young, eager lawyer, with whom he was happy.

The big animal seemed refreshed by his night of rest, but Thorne was still feeling far from recovered from his long day as he trailed along the road at the top of the valley. Keeping Avery's eatery in sight, he was pleased to see the trim form of Abbey Watt atop her dark mare coming towards him. She seemed to be like him in one aspect of her personality: she did not waste any time, only he had a feeling that the deal they were going to make was a lot more urgent in her case than his.

Tom Bate was not waiting for them when they went into the wide-open pass, even though they had made an arrangement. While Abbey waited on her mount Thorne went into the ranch to investigate. The old man was lying on a sheepskin rug in front of the fireplace, near the cold ashes of what must have once been a roaring fire, with arms outspread. At first Thorne thought he was dead and his heart sank to his boots — not just for his own sake, but that of his new neighbour, Abbey — but an empty bottle lying nearby told its own story. The old man had celebrated well last night.

Thorne finally got him awake with the help of some cold water and a promise of food once they got into town. The three of them rode into Brewlins while it was still early in the morning, the old man sagging in the saddle. Thorne had to help him dismount before they hitched their horses at the post outside the lawyer's office.

'Who are we seeing?' Abbey asked as they came down the hills into town.

'Justin Bowers,' said Thorne. 'I picked his name off a shingle I saw in town.'

'Why him in particular?'

'You'll think it odd, but I just got a feeling this would be someone we could use.'

'Then your feeling is correct. He's one of the few not in the pocket of the cattlemen.'

Justin Bowers was a tall, good-looking young man with butter-coloured hair. He did not actually rub his hands together when they came into his office, but his toothy smile was welcoming in the extreme. Business, it was obvious to see, was not good. They told him what they wanted. Abbey required a transfer of the brand to her name and she also wanted to purchase the remaining cattle. Thorne explained that he wanted a far more difficult transaction, the purchase of the ranch from the retiring owner. Bowers was more than willing.

'Well, all three of you are here, so we can put the processes in motion.'

'We want it done now,' said Thorne.

'Let me explain a minor problem,' said Bowers frankly. 'If you want me to arrange for a transfer of freehold and land to you right now, it will take time because documents have to be drawn up and signed. The bill of sale for the brand and the cattle will take less time.'

'Then do hers first,' said Thorne. 'Do mine as well, but make it one big transaction.'

'That will also cost a good deal of money and, quite frankly, I don't know if you have the sums involved.'

'While you're doing the paperwork for the lady, I'll get a wire sent from my bank that shows I have sufficient funds,' said Thorne.

'I'll pay my own way, thank you,' said

Abbey Watt firmly.

'Let him do this,' piped up Old Tom unexpectedly, 'he's trying to help you both. When your side is done you can be on your way.' Not wanting to displease the old man, who might pull out of the deal, she subsided.

'This is the boring bit for us all,' said Bowers. 'I have to sit with my clerk and draw up the documents, and not just one copy either, but copies for us all.' He looked sharply at Thorne. 'If you don't mind, I'd like some kind of payment upfront.'

'I thought that might be the case.' Thorne casually reached into his deep pockets, took out a handful of gold eagles and laid them on the desk. 'Is that enough to get you started?'

'Sure is; I'll get to business,' said Bowers.

'Then what will we do?' asked Abbey.

'Take Tom here for his breakfast,' said Thorne. Bowers agreed that this was a good idea and they went out into Fuller Street, where the office was located.

There was a nearby eatery called 'The Food Stop', to which he escorted them before going to the telegraph office on his own business. He soon had a wire that showed he had plenty of funds in the bank. He could get some of it transferred to the old man. He went out of the telegraph office to go back to the lawyer's office and saw a sight that would have chilled the heart of all but the most fearless individual.

Wingate and three other men were on their steeds in the middle of Fuller Street. They were all armed, and as Jubal appeared Wingate drew his coat aside to reveal more starkly the gleam of the weapon at his side. Thorne recognized the whiskered man from the previous day and the two others looked vaguely familiar as well. They were clearly out to intimidate him, having learned that he was back in town, but Jubal went straight to the lawyer's office with the telegram safely tucked into his breast pocket.

Along with the help of his office boy, Bowers had been working hard and the transfer of the brand and the cattle document was ready. The deeds were taking a little while longer, but luckily Old Tom had brought in his original document, which had probably been tucked behind a firebrick in his mantle for forty years, and that gave them something to work with.

'I'll be another half hour with this one,' said Bowers.

'That's all right, I'll go and get my companions,' said Thorne, 'and then we can get all signed up.'

He went back out to the main street. Wingate and his men were still there, the set look on their faces of people who had come to do a job.

'Howdy, Mr Thorne,' said Wingate. 'You got some business going on?'

'Anything I'm doing is my business,' said Thorne evenly. He refrained from adding *and none of yours*, although the thought ran through his mind. He left them and went to the food place where his companions were waiting. The thought was in his mind that he should refrain from telling them what was going on, but he had an idea in his head.

'Is there a back entrance to this place?' he asked a startled Abbey.

'I guess so, what's going on?'

'Seems that you can't carry out a straight transaction in this town,' said Thorne evenly, 'without someone turning up to rubberneck you doing so.'

'They're out there, aren't they?' said Tom. 'I'll just go straight out and tell 'em what I think. Bunch of lamebrained buzzards.'

'I don't think so,' said Thorne. 'Discretion is the better part of valour as they say.' He sized up the food place with an expert eye. 'If we get out the back, we can knock on the lawyer's back door and no one will see Abbey.'

'Why should I skulk about my own town?' she demanded.

'Because I have a feeling there's some gunpowder out there in the shape of Wingate and his men,' said Thorne evenly, 'and I think you'll be the fire that sets the touch paper alight.'

'The hell with them, I'll do what I want,' she said, her eyes blazing with fury.

Thorne said the only thing that would have made her respond at that second. 'Then you risk losing your brand and everything that follows.' That news silenced her.

'All right, I'll do it.'

It wasn't long before they were out at the back of the building. The lawyer's office was three doors down.

'I'll go out front and I'll get past them,' said Thorne, 'then I'll get Bowers to shout you.' Luckily for them, after a brief explanation, the owner of the food shop, who had known Abbey, had agreed to cooperate as long as he wasn't dragged into any kind of conflict.

Thorne strolled out the front again and into the lawyer's office. The four riders were still there, but he could see they were ready to dismount at the slightest hint that they were being crossed in any way. Thorne closed the door behind him, pulled down the shade and spoke to a startled Bowers. 'Let them in, they're at the back.'

Bowers did as he was asked, without asking questions, which was a good sign. Old Tom and the woman came in.

'Let's get these documents signed,' said Thorne. 'Once that's done we can think of a way of getting out of here.'

The deeds were signed by the Old Man, who gave a deep sigh. 'Guess that's just part of my life that's over,' he said. 'I'll miss it in a lot of ways, but not the winters; they was getting harder and harder.'

'Right,' said Abbey briskly, tucking the transfer documents for the brand well down into her bosom. 'Now all we have to do is get out of here.'

'That won't be hard,' said Thorne. 'I'll draw them off and you just get to the livery, fetch your animals, and ride the hell out of town.'

'Well, it's been a pleasure doing business,' said Bowers. 'Not quite what I expected though.'

Thorne made sure the woman and

the older man were away out the back, going towards the livery. Then he went back inside and thanked Bowers again, and went outside.

'What are you up to?' snarled Wingate as he appeared again.

'Reckon that's my business,' said Thorne. He knew the men were jumpy, that the situation could turn into a shootout in seconds, but he had to appear defiant to win time for the others.

He could feel the comforting weight of his guns in his pockets as he faced up to all four.

8

In the meantime Abbey Watt and her companion were making their way towards the livery, glad that they had left their steeds there earlier instead of leaving them in town. The back of the main street was littered with all kinds of rubbish: discarded boards, broken rain barrels and even heaps of food debris that owners flung out of their windows when they were finished eating. Old Tom complained all the time under his breath about his aching back and kept muttering the word 'whippersnappers' to himself. At one point, when he barked his shins against something, he gave a shout of annoyance and Abbey froze, thinking that they would have been heard. But they were far enough away from the four riders that the sound was not heard in the general bustle of a town waking up for the day. They got to the livery and liberated their horses, leading them away from the building until they were not visible from the main street, and rode out of town.

Abbey took one backwards glance at the town where there was a man who was helping her out for reasons she could not fathom, and then spurred her mare onwards behind Tom's blue as they rode back to his ranch.

Once they got there she counted out the two hundred dollars she owed him for the brand and he fetched not one iron, but two that he had kept carefully hidden in the back room of the ranch. He handed them over to her with the look of a man who was giving away part of his life.

'Can't say the money won't be useful, and you bought these fair an' square. Look after 'em and get a copy made at Joe's in town. He's a good blacksmith, made these for me when the others got worn.'

She thanked him and kissed him on his leathery old cheeks. He smiled for the first time.

'Reckon I'll rest these aching bones then finish off my arrangements. A couple of days and I'll be gone. I'll miss the place, it's been my life.'

'You're better off with family, Tom,' she said. 'It's been long overdue. Now, to get to business, I'll send Cy and Billy to fetch the cattle. They'll be here in another day or so. You know them, so you'll be fine with that.'

'I guess so.'

Abbey took the irons, which had been wrapped in buckskin, and rode away from the ranch. Things were finally going her way and it didn't even matter if the irons were somehow taken from her on the way back because she was the legal owner of the Lazy B brand — she could make as many copies as she wanted. It was another blow against Stryker and his kind.

But as she rode for home, her long hair streaming from under her wide-brimmed hat, she could not help turning her thoughts to Thorne. She already owed him so much.

Thorne stood with his legs apart and his hands at his side as he faced the four horsemen. He was more frightened of the horses than the men, truth to tell, because it would be easy enough for them to ride over him and claim it was an accident.

'You boys don't want to start trouble,' he said.

'Why would you want to visit a lawyer?' asked Wingate.

'I guess that's my business,' said Thorne. 'Why would you want to stop me?'

'See, a man comes to a place an' knows nothing,' said Wingate, 'ain't that right, partners?'

'Sure is,' said the whiskered man, who was called Venters.

'See, along with the boys here, we think your coming here is mighty strange,' said Wingate, 'so you just watch what you're doing.'

'I'll follow the law, like you should,'

said Thorne, gazing at them long and hard. Despite the almost wispy quality about the tall, lean man enveloped in his big coat, there was something hard and defiant about Thorne that worried the four men facing him. Wingate suddenly stopped talking and looked around.

'This ain't getting us anywhere. You just watch what you're doing, Thorne. Ride, boys.'

But just as the four began to spur their mounts on, a gun appeared in both of Thorne's hands as if by magic. 'Try and ride over me and you'll face the consequences.'

It was the excuse Wingate had been looking for. He jumped off his mount and the others followed suit, pulling his Smith & Wesson revolver from his holster as he did so.

'Get him, boys, he's attacked us.' Thorne felt a sense of regret that it had come to this, that there would soon be four dead men littering the street, but in this world deeds spoke first. They thought they had him, but he was like a feline ready to pounce with a speed and dexterity that would not be believed even when it happened.

The whole event was brought to a halt by a loud shotgun blast that went over everyone's heads. The horses started bucking and whinnying so that the men had to holster up to grab their reins and calm them down, although Wingate still levelled his weapon. Matt Buck came striding towards them, holding the still-smoking gun in his hands.

'That's enough; I'll have no gun law on my streets.'

'This miscreant attacked us,' said Wingate. 'Ain't that right boys?'

'They were going to ride over me,' said Thorne, who was now barehanded, the Peacemakers having disappeared as magically as when they had arrived.

'I saw everything,' said Buck, 'and like the man said, you were going to ride him down.'

'We'll see what happens in future,'

Wingate stared levelly into Thorne's face. 'There won't be a friendly sheriff around the next time we meet.' He and his men departed, and Thorne stood there for a moment watching them leave. He won plenty of time for Abbey Watt but he had made a certain enemy. He hoped it was worth the price.

★ ★ ★

Stryker was back at his own ranch when the men arrived back from town. He had spotted Thorne riding up to the Bate place the previous day and he had guessed that the former gunman was going to attempt to buy the ranch. He had also guessed that Thorne would need the services of a lawyer. Luckily his men had been sent out to get the fencing done, so he had gone to fetch them and they had ridden into town to confront the new arrival and perhaps scare him off. When the men arrived back at the 'big house', as they liked to call his ranch, he was in the yard. He could not appear to be against the arrival of new people and he could palm off the behaviour of his men as just natural rivalry if need be.

Nothing to do with a wealthy landowner.

The men rode into the yard, Wingate with a face like stone. They were soon gathered around their commander. For three of them it had been a welcome break from the fencing, which was hard work, but for Wingate it was a personal defeat he was not taking lightly.

'Well, did you scare him off?' said Stryker, keeping a light tone.

'He was quaking in his boots,' replied Wingate. 'We had him frightened as hell, didn't we boys?' Not wanting to look bad the other three mumbled an agreement, but Big Sutter, as usual, did not manage to make his reply very convincing.

'So he's warned off now and he won't be trying to do anything in this territory?'

'Not exactly boss.' Wingate searched

carefully for the right words. 'We got him to draw on us, and we was about to deal with it legally when Matt Buck spoiled the fun.'

'Buck?' Stryker's face tightened. 'He's had it in for me ever since I won Lilly Belle off him fair and square. I had land and money, he had the possibility of being under a headstone, job he's in, and she made the right choice.'

'Upshot is, Thorne's still around but there's something mighty strange going on.' Wingate rubbed his pointed chin thoughtfully. 'Can't swear to it but it was as if he was stalling us.'

'Stalling four riders? He's got balls of steel then. Where was he when you got him?'

'See that's the strange thing, he was in at a lawyer's office.'

Stryker was still in business because he could put together facts more quickly than your average man, and he was not about to let this one get away.

'A lawyer? He wouldn't go and see a lawyer unless he was getting some kind of bill of sale. The hell with it, he's moved quickly. Was there anyone else with him?'

'Not that we saw.'

'Then he was stalling you, stalling you until the other one got away, and I know just who that other one was. Tom Bate, that devious old bastard.'

'What should we do now?'

'Nothing right now, there's nothing we can do without drawing the eye of Buck after your public behaviour. What was the lawyer called?'

'Bowers.'

'Wait, I know him. He was after some railway contracts a few months ago and didn't get them. He's needing the work.' Stryker became silent as he always did when he was working something out in his head. At last he looked at the three men. 'You, Sutter, Venters and Lewis, get back to work. The job won't get done unless you take it in hand.' The three men looked fairly rebellious. They had been drafted in by Wingate for a particular task, they were not looking forward to having to go back down to Clearwater Valley; it was a long ride for more back breaking toil.

'It's like this, boys,' said Stryker. 'The government ain't doin' right by us with this Homesteading Act of theirs. They let in a bunch of greenhorns and conmen that've come here to take over land that was once used by us for our ranching. Them meadows down there are all that keeps us solvent during the hot summer months when the grass dries and withers on what little plains we have around here, and the autumn harvest is where we get the bales for our winter feed. You know what? You are preserving your jobs by doin' this, and you'll get a nice little bonus at the end.'

This rousing speech was more than enough to cheer the men. It wasn't long before they departed in much better spirits, particularly since Stryker gave them an allowance out of his own pocket to spend at the saloon store on what they liked.

Once Stryker was with his companion he became serious again.

'Well, looks like we got a job ahead of us. I'll get in touch with the railroad people and get Bowers a contract that takes him away completely.'

'Will he take it?'

'He'd be foolish not to, given it'll make him enough money to keep his business on an even keel, but it will mean travelling to the headquarters in another state. That will happen today.'

'Then what?' Stryker looked at Wingate steadily.

'I think we know each other well enough. You know what to do.'

9

Thorne returned to the Brewlins Hotel. He had not made his connection with Abbey Watt clear, so he was quite surprised when he heard her name being mentioned by a statuesque young woman in the reception area. She was dressed in a flowing green dress, and had upswept hair with a peacock feather in it. She was speaking to the older man who had booked Thorne in.

'I wouldn't be here without Abbey Watt.' She became aware that Thorne was gazing at her. 'I beg your pardon, sir,' she said. Thorne doffed his hat to her.

'Name's Thorne, just staying here a few days while I get set up. Couldn't help hearing a name I recognized.' She looked at him with an air of distrust.

'This is our housekeeper,' said the reception clerk, Frank, who also happened to be the owner of the hotel.

'Housekeeper' did not mean someone who did domestic work such as cooking and cleaning: the title was an honorific for someone who made sure that the hotel was run smoothly, and included everything from ordering in fresh food to taking care of the books.

'Lena McDonald,' said the woman reluctantly. 'I'd rather not discuss Abbey Watt with you, Mr Thorne. I have work to do.' She began to turn away in a pointed manner.

'Wait a minute,' said Thorne, 'I have a personal interest in Miss Watt.'

'I'm sure you do.' She would have been an attractive woman if she had been smiling but her mouth was serious and her brow furrowed. 'I really have to go.'

'I just want to know a little bit more about your friend,' said Thorne, 'and then maybe I'll be in a position to help her in the future.'

'I beg your pardon,' said the young woman, 'but you don't look as if you are here to help anyone but yourself.'

'Well you're wrong: it's in my interests to know about the town and the area because I've just bought the Bate spread, and Miss Watt was with me when I did it because she got the brand she's been looking for.'

'Frank, can you excuse us?' said Lena. 'I need to speak with this customer alone.'

'Fine,' said the owner, 'but I'll not hear a word said against Abbey Watt, and what they're saying about this hotel. I just get angry.'

She led Thorne into the bar area and poured him a whiskey. He reached into his pocket to get his payment, but she dismissed the gesture with a wave of her hand.

'If what you're saying is true, and I believe you somehow, then you and Abbey are both still in danger. She came here from Arkansas eight years ago.'

'What, with her family?'

'No, that's the remarkable thing. She was quite alone. She lit up at the Brewlins hotel where she became a cook, a waiter and a fine seamstress. Her work was much in demand by the towns-women and she made good money. Frank wanted to travel, so he eventually made her the housekeeper. I was a maid then, very young, I'll never forget her many kindnesses towards me.'

'Sounds like she had a good deal here, why would she leave?'

'Because she met Merrill Avery.'

'I've met him too; he seems quite a go-getter.'

'Avery had his own ranch out in Clearwater Valley. But he found it hard to make a living with cattle because of the big boys. They made it harder and harder to buy at auctions. But he was married, with a young wife. I didn't get to know her because it all happened when I was a child. Such a tragedy.'

'What happened to her?'

'She was pregnant with her first child, there was no real medical help around and she got the childbed fever and died. They say Merrill was lost without her. He lost all his cattle and he was all set to go bankrupt, although luckily he owned the land because he had bought it with the profits he made when he first settled here.'

'So where does Abbey Watt come into this?'

'She met Merrill because he came into town and began drinking here. He was different from the cowboys who came here and tried to impress her, he was older, and steadier. It was Abbey who saw the potential in his ranch. She knew it was right there at the head of the valley, on the Oregon Trail. She saw at once that he had the potential to make a lot of money.'

'With the eatery you mean?'

'It's a shop too, around the back, selling everything from tobacco to whiskey. She told him what to do, even offered to loan him some money at the time, but on condition that he cut her in for a share of the profits and gave her a job.'

'And the eatery's been successful?'

'They're not the richest people around here — you have to look at the cattle barons for that — but they've made a pretty penny or two.'

'You say 'they' as if they're more than partners.'

'I'm not saying a thing.' Lena looked at him a little slyly and he realized that she did not entirely trust him. He did not blame her, because if their positions had been reversed he would have been reluctant to speak to a stranger about such things.

'I'll tell you what's going on,' he said. 'Avery was able to carry on his business unmolested for the last eight years, with Abbey Watt as his investor and worker. The valley was used by cattlemen going to market, and by the local cattlemen for a source of rich feed. Just lately those relationships have soured because Abbey Watt — legally, under the Homesteading Act — established her own claim.'

'See, when you say things like that it makes me alarmed,' said the girl stiffly, beginning to rise.

'No, don't.' His voice had an air of authority and she sat down again, but with a taut manner about her that said she would flee in an instant.

'Miss Watt has staked out her claim and she's getting in the way of Stryker and his friends at the Cattle Trading Association.'

'They're saying horrible things about her,' burst out Lena. 'They're saying that this was a bawdy house, that she was a prostitute — only they use the word 'whore'. They say worse, that she's a cattle rustler, that the couple of dozen she's got aren't hers, but she says she bought them from herders passing through, legally enough. This was never a whorehouse; I took over from Abbey, and she trained me. They're horrible people, horrible.' She burst into tears.

Thorne did not say anything. He was beginning to realize that he had walked into a situation that had been brewing for a long time. As the young woman dabbed at her eyes he remained calm and began to rise from his seat.

'Thanks for telling me what you know.'

'There's more than that.' It seemed that he had opened a floodgate in the young woman.

'What do you mean?'

'You didn't ask me why she was here on her own.'

'It was the first thing I thought of, but it's none of my business.' To tell the truth he was curious about why a good-looking woman like Abbey Watt had made a new start in a strange place when most women of her age and looks would have been married a long time ago.

'When she lived in Kansas she was married to a man called Latimer.'

'So she's a married woman after all.'

'Not now. You see Latimer was an agent for a bottled goods company. He didn't know where she had gone to when she left him. He came here looking for business and he found out that she was working for Merrill.'

'So he tried to get back with her?'

'He wasn't very good to her when they were married. I heard a lot of things she said when she had the odd drink and she let it slip. He used to hit her quite a lot, and her father, who was a bully of a man, who got money from Latimer, told her she just had to obey her husband when she first reported the beatings. That's why she ran away from him and started a new life here.'

Now Abbey Watt's story made more sense to Thorne. It was hard for a woman to make her way in a world where men had most of the power.

'So, did she get her divorce?'

'In a manner of speaking. Latimer turned up and said he was there to claim his wife, and he wasn't going to let old Avery stop him from doing so.'

'I'm guessing that there was some kind of fight?'

The girl looked at him sharply. 'Are you making a fool of me?'

'No,' said Thorne shortly. 'Go on.'

'Latimer was a bully who picked on those who he thought was weaker than him. But Merrill Avery is much tougher than he looks. There was a fight, and instead of the younger man beating him, Avery broke Latimer's neck.'

'So Avery has been arraigned for murder?'

'Well, the fight took place at the eatery, in front of plenty of witnesses, and it was Latimer who picked it in the first place, he struck the first blow, so Avery got off with a plea of self-defence. Latimer was buried five years ago, but nobody has forgotten what happened.'

'Well if Abbey is a widow, what's to stop her marrying Avery?'

'I don't know. She doesn't talk about it, but I think she saw another side of Avery that day, and it was one she didn't like even though she hated her husband.'

'Well, it's all over now,' said Thorne, 'but thanks, Lena, for giving me the low-down on the CTA and Abbey Watt. I guess there's a lot more to this situation than I thought.' He stood up again, tipped his hat to her and began to walk away.

'Mr Thorne,' she said.

'Yes?' He turned back.

'Watch out for Stryker. He's a bad man.'

'I already am.' He moved forward again, feeling that tingling between his shoulder blades that told him this was far from over.

10

Cy and Billy were roughly the same age, both fifteen years old. Given that her ranch had only three workers beside herself, Abbey Watt had a lot of work to do to keep the place going. When she got back to the ranch, the first thing she did was to summon the two boys and let them know about her latest purchase.

'Tom has two-dozen head of cattle. I want you boys to go to his spread and fetch them. Bring them back here.'

'But they'll have his brand on them,' said Billy, a tall, well-built lad with long, dark hair. He looked as if he might have a touch of Indian blood in him.

'That's all right,' said Abbey, 'because as from now we're the owners of the Lazy B brand.' She showed them the irons and the documents.

'Does this mean we'll keep our jobs?'

asked Cyrus. He was big and broad-shouldered, as fair as Billy was dark. Avery had once employed his father, but that was in the early days. His father was no more and, like Billy, he was an orphan.

'That's exactly right.'

'But how are you going to feed all the cattle with Mr Stryker fencing in the land?'

'There's plenty of land and plenty of feed down here,' said Abbey. 'Let me worry about that when the time comes. Now get going.'

The two boys rode out on their pie-balds towards the Bate spread. It would be a task getting the cattle down to the valley, but if Old Tom could do it on his own they would be able to handle the task, and finally start to become real cowpunchers. They were at an age where they were filled with boundless energy and they pushed their horses hard to get to the ranch, laughing and joking with each other on the way.

'What do you whippersnappers want?' asked Tom on their arrival. He was looking fresher than before. He had trimmed his whiskers, had a good wash and changed his clothes to a sedate dark shirt, black trousers and shiny boots that had never seen the light of day before.

'Miss Abbey sent us. She's asked us to fetch the cattle,' said Billy.

'Well, guess I'll help you round 'em up and get 'em out,' said the old man, 'but you'll excuse me if I don't come down the valley with you. It's a long ride and these old bones creak too much.' Although he had barely met either of the boys before, he immediately believed their story because he knew that Abbey Wart had taken them in due to circumstances beyond their control.

Although the young men were not that experienced, they had already worked with cattle down at Abbey's ranch and twenty-four was no number to handle. All they had to do was find a leader — which they did in one formidable beast who seemed to catch the scent of the sweet, fresh grass in the valley off them — and the herd would trail with her. Besides, once they were on the main path to the valley the animals, who were far from stupid, would catch the knowledge of the thousands of animals that had come that way before and they would be quite willing to continue.

Old Tom stood at the road to his ranch and said goodbye to the two young men, waving to them as they went. He was no longer smiling as he turned to go into his ranch with his shoulders slumped.

'What's wrong with him?' asked Billy. Cyrus, who was a lot more perceptive than his companion, made a stab at an answer.

'I guess he's been here most of his life, now he's seeing the final part of that life leaving in the shape of these here cows.'

This meant little or nothing to Billy who was not the most perceptive of young men.

'I guess so,' he mumbled.

They came out of the pass and

allowed the cattle to amble down the hill towards the wide trail. They were met by Wingate and Lewis. Wingate had an unpleasant sneer on his face as he looked at them.

'Starting the drive a bit early ain't we?'

'Never mind him, Billy,' said Cy.

'You taking these to market for Old Tom? Didn't know he employed children,' said Wingate.

'These ain't Tom's no more,' began Billy hotly, when Cy gave him a warning glare.

'Billy, don't say another word. It ain't your business, Mr Wingate.'

'Might be,' said Wingate. 'What do you think, Jim?'

'I think these here cattle are Old Tom's,' said Lewis thoughtfully. 'Matter of fact, I think I recognize some from the auction that was held in town last spring.'

'So, what's happened here is you've got Tom to sell you the last of his stock,' said Wingate, the smile now completely gone as he rubbed at his chin. The sneering smile returned. 'That means that the goddamned whore you're employed by has won her a little game.'

''Taint none of your business,' said Cy stoutly. 'Now get out of our way.' Both of the older riders were armed, but the only weapons the boys had were their Bowie knives, quirts for directing the horses and cattle, and a stick each. If the two older men cut up rough, then they wouldn't have much chance. Also Billy had a temper, as was shown by the tide of crimson creeping up over his neck and face and he was liable to let that temper explode at any minute.

'It's real fortunate for you that we're busy,' said Wingate. 'Just let the bitch know, a few more cattle here nor there won't make no difference to what happens in the end. She ain't got a valid claim, and I'm taking my own claim serious.' The two men rode off.

'I'll kill them,' said Billy furiously. This was not their only encounter with the two men, who had been supervising

102

in the fencing of land near Abbey's claim. Billy did not respond well to being needled.

'You'll get these back to the ranch, along with me,' said Cy. 'Come on.' They ambled along their way, but any pleasure that they might have been taking out of their little adventure had been destroyed. Now it was just a job from which they wanted to get back as soon as possible. The cows as usual went at a pace all of their own, and were soon cropping the fresh green grass of the valley in a field beside their new companions.

★ ★ ★

Stryker listened thoughtfully to what his men had to say.

'I knew there was a chance Tom was going to sell up, but I didn't think it would happen so quickly. So Thorne's already done the deed? Well, it's time for me to get my part of the job done.'

'Not going to affect us much, Abbey

Watt having a few more head of cattle,' said Jim Lewis.

'That's where you ain't thinking,' said Stryker. 'If she goes on with what she's doing, she'll think that she has a right to continue. Don't you get what she's up to?'

'I don't see it,' said Lewis.

'Business ain't what it used to be,' said Stryker. 'In any business there's a bottom line. We're facing a lot of problems, and this Homesteading Act is a real pain in our butts. If we let Abbey Watt succeed she's just the thin end of the wedge. If she gets in, then others will follow. Strictly speaking, Dabs, if they challenge your claim — the one that you say is yours anyway — they wouldn't find it too hard to fight in court.'

'That won't happen, they don't have the money, boss.'

'Well, that's the thing, if enough of 'em get together with an idealistic young lawyer, say, they could well win that kind of case, showing that the land interest is really mine. That could reflect in the interests of the business real bad.'

'It ain't as if it's just her,' said Wingate. 'We all know that she's a lying whore and that she's been with Avery for years. She didn't just work for him, she worked with him, and at least half that business of his really belongs to her.'

'And she just filed the claim on that land a few months ago,' said Stryker. 'She'd set the cabin up there two years previous, and you know as well as I do that under the law she's entitled to claim that land as hers, but it ain't hers.'

'I don't see what you mean.'

'You think Avery's got nothing to do with this? In his soul do you really think he likes serving eats to a bunch of rough riders? Hell no, he was born a herder, it's part of what he is and this repeal is going to help him, and others like him no end.'

'What repeal is that, boss?'

Stryker gave a look of annoyance that had nothing to do with Wingate.

'They're repealing the Maverick Act.'

'Now that ain't fair.'

'That act was brought in for a reason. Too many unmarked calves were being taken by those who didn't have a right to have 'em.'

'You mean like Abbey Watt?'

'Well, she wasn't around at the time, but basically the members of the Cattle Trading Association got together and got a law passed by the Territory — the Maverick Possession Act — that stated any member who found an unmarked calf could brand it as his own. The way things are, some of us would be up one season while others would be up the next, but it all evened out in the end. Only the cattle traders within the organisation could do it; anyone else trying would become a criminal.'

'Seem to remember that it took a lynching or three to sort out who owned what,' said Jim Lewis with a touch of unseemly relish at the thought.

'So you think the repeal will hurt us?' asked Wingate.

'Dead right it will. If that woman and

others who've set up their homesteads in this area find an unmarked animal, they'll be able to brand it as their own, not to mention being able to sell it at market price. You let this rabble in, prices will fall, and the next thing you know we'll have to get rid of men, land and cattle just to make ends meet.'

Given that Stryker had one of the biggest ranches in the area, stock holdings that were more extensive than most men in the district, and a huge bank balance, Wingate seriously doubted if this was the case. Men and animals might have to go, but Stryker was already so well off it wouldn't really affect him that badly on a personal basis.

'She's got to be stopped,' said Stryker. 'She really is the thin end of the wedge. If she gets away with what she's doing they'll all crowd in, you know that's a fact. As for Tom selling up — well, a man has to have a lawyer to prove that kind of thing.'

'But don't Bowers have a partner of some kind?'

'No, he's just set up in town. He has an office boy who does all his writing — but the boy has gone off with him to do this work for the railway company.'

'Already?'

'Well, Bowers was offered a fair amount to sort out those articles of legislation for the railroad. He's going to be away for a good long time.'

'You sure know how to get things going, boss,' said Wingate admiringly.

'Maybe I do, but let's make sure this Thorne doesn't get too uppity,' said Stryker.

'Well, boss, we've done it before. We'll do it again,' said Wingate.

They had no time to waste.

11

Jubal Thorne looked at his assembled goods, which were not great: his tobacco pouch, his knife, his Winchester '73, and his two Peacemakers laid out on the bed. He had the bedroll he had slept in during his trip from Arizona and a few items of clothing, including spare boots and the clothes he stood up in. The few items left over were on his iron-framed hotel bed. It was early the next morning and he had a job to do. Everything had been arranged. He was going to escort the old man to the railway station and Tom would begin the long haul back to the east.

The two men had hit it off well. Now they were parting just when they were becoming friends, and Thorne would be sleeping on a harder bed tonight. He bagged what few goods he had, putting what he could into his pockets and holding the bedroll under his arm.

On the way out of the room he bumped into the young woman, Lena, with whom he had conversed the previous day.

'So you're on your way?' she asked.

'Time for me to start a new life,' said Thorne.

'Why did you come here?' asked Lena. 'Don't you have a family, friends, and a life elsewhere?'

'I have one brother left,' said Thorne, 'he farms out in a place further south.'

'But what about a woman, a wife, children of your own?'

'I have to get going,' said Thorne with what he hoped was an easygoing smile, 'we have an early start.' The young woman sensed that she had struck a raw nerve somewhere, but she didn't know where.

'Just keep an eye on what's happening around here, and don't believe a word they say about Abbey or anyone else.'

'I make up my own mind,' he told her. She was close to him now and he could sense warmth between them that had not been there when they had first spoken to each other.

'Well if you need my help in any way, let me know.' She had a scent of fresh soap and perfume about her and she was prettier when she smiled than he had seen the day before. She leaned in and suddenly kissed him on the good side of his face.

'What was that for?'

'I have a sense of what people are,' said Lena. 'You look as if you could be a dangerous man, but I sense some real learning in you, an education. You're not just some kind of ex-bounty hunter.'

'Well, miss, thanks for that ringing endorsement, but I guess I'll be on my way.'

As he came out of the hotel and went to fetch Eb from the livery, he noticed that the town was already busy. The presence of the railway and the movement of goods including materials and cattle meant that Brewlins was always busy during the week. With coalmines and a quarry nearby, there was plenty of work in the area and work meant settlers, who would make the town expand rapidly.

There only seemed to be one exception to this rule. As he rode through Fuller Street he noticed that the offices of Justin Bowers were locked against the outside world. This might be because the young lawyer had not yet started work, but in a place like this where people started early and finished late a young go-getter like Bowers was not likely to be missing from his place of work.

Unless he had business that would take him elsewhere.

The thought crossed Thorne's mind that he and Abbey had been lucky to catch the young lawyer when he was not busy, if that was the case. Thorne thought back to the events of the previous day. He had taken a risk of antagonising his new neighbours in the ranching business, but he had also stood up for what he believed in. He was not in the habit of backing down when he thought he was in the right, and Wingate had been bluffing, of that Thorne was sure.

Thorne rode out of town towards the road that led up to his ranch. His thoughts were dwelling on Lena and the extraordinary way she had taken to him. She was a young, strong-minded woman of the type he liked. She reminded him of a younger, less caustic version of Abbey Watt. As he urged his steed onwards, though not galloping him on the rocky terrain, Thorne allowed his thoughts to dwell on a possible future with the young woman. It was not without the bounds of possibility that she might want the kind of security offered by an older man.

There was another thought in the back of his mind about what had happened the last time he had tried the same thing, but it was a thought he pushed away as soon as it came to the fore.

Thorne came to the pass that led to

the property that was now his. Unlike Tom and other settlers, he was not interested in raising cattle. This was not a job for which he felt he was suited. His aim was quite simple, to establish stables up here in the hills and supply all those who needed his services a particular type of horse for their work. He liked horses, had the talent for training them, and the practical ability to deal with a breeding programme.

He was well aware that he would not make a fortune at the trade, but he had an idea that such a business would tick over nicely and make a reasonable profit from year to year without making its owner rich.

That was when thoughts of Lena came in again. She seemed a practical woman, a good housekeeper, and running a hotel was not an easy job. She would be an asset to the business. 'And elsewhere,' he said out loud, grinning a little as he thought of how pretty she was.

He arrived at the ranch, dismounted

from his horse and led him forward. There was an air of neglect about the place that was even more marked now that there was a distinct lack of stock. Tom's horse was there, a big grey, indifferently cropping some grass in the nearby corral. He should have been saddled and ready, but Thorne could picture what would have happened the previous night. Tom would have celebrated his last night here in fine style with a bottle of good whiskey.

'Miss Watt must have sent her boys up to fetch the cattle just like she said she would,' Thorne told Eb who twitched his ears indifferently. It was not the warmest of mornings, and up here the wind soughed and there was a cold breeze. Thorne shivered even though he was wearing a thick coat. There was a sudden squall and rain pattered down on the worn shingles of the roof.

'Tom, are you there?' asked Thorne as he climbed the steps and up to the porch that was now his. He felt a distinct heat between his shoulder blades and, without thinking about what he was doing, went into bounty hunter mode. He pulled out his twin Peacemakers, holding them ready, pulled back and listened for movement from within. The rain pattered down, but there was no other sound as he waited and the slow seconds ticked away.

'Tom?' he demanded. 'Tom, are you there?'

At last, trusting to his instincts, he moved stealthily into the building. Tom was in the main room, just where Thorne had expected to find him. There was an empty bottle of whiskey at the old man's side, and he was sprawled on the ground. Only Tom wasn't dead drunk, as Thorne had expected.

Tom was just plain dead, with a bullet hole square in the middle of his chest.

12

Abbey Watt looked around her ranch. This was the scene of her greatest triumph, she was the owner of one hundred and sixty acres of land, all of which she had fenced in with the help of Cyrus, his father, and the two boys, who had both been thirteen when they had started the Herculean task just two years ago. She was wearing a long, dark skirt and a green blouse. As usual she wore leather boots with square heels that made her seem taller than she was, and her hair was tied back in a long, raven black ponytail.

She had her own livery with plenty of horses housed inside; there was a barn, several smaller outbuildings and the ranch itself. She looked on the ranch with pride. This had started off as a small cabin that she and Avery had built there with their own hands in that not-so-distant time before. It had literally been one room, in which she had put a bed and an iron stove, a few prints on the walls and nothing else. Now the ranch extended well to either side of the original cabin. There was a roomy porch out front and a kitchen extension at the back.

There was only one problem that she could see. Avery, who turned up to see her by riding down from the head of the valley on his blue, pinpointed the issue even as he slid off his mount.

'Mornin', Abbey.' He did not so much come towards her, kiss her or even lay a hand on her in any way. They took no chances when it came to what they had made. 'I see right away what they've done. Bastards,' he added.

Just beyond the corrals that they had so painstakingly constructed — the cattle being kept further up — there was a stretch of land that should have been green pasture. There was a small cabin further away that had been so crudely constructed that it would not have been fit for human habitation. All of the land around this had been enclosed by lightly made wood and wire fencing.

'This was your pasture,' said Avery, 'they can't do this.'

'Well, they have done it, and filed a claim of their own under that snake Wingate.'

'There's nothing we can do about it,' said Avery. Then he saw that her expression had become a little fixed. He knew that look; he had seen it many times during their life together such as it had been.

'Abbey, no, I can see what you're thinking. We've discussed this before.'

'Sure you can, and it would be us that would be in the right,' she said in a flat voice that said she was not going to argue with him. 'I've got Punch; maybe I'll let him earn his keep.'

Punch was the big draught animal that she kept on her land. He was housed in the livery with the rest but dwarfed them with his big black-and-white frame, and his huge hoofs with a fringe of white hair around each. He ate more than the rest of the horses, nearly twice as much in fact, but he was immensely strong. She had bought him at auction when he was a foal, seeing the potential in an animal most smallholders would have avoided due to the amount of food he would eat and the amount of care he would need.

'If you're talking about ploughing, and you're attaching him to the plough, then you'll be doing well,' said Avery. 'You need to grow oats for the winter, but if you're thinking of going about this in some other way, please don't.' There was a plea in his voice that she could not ignore.

'Merrill, don't forget we're in the right. They've come down here and taken over my meadows. My claim is legitimate as you well know.'

'Then let's take them to court.' But she was as dismissive of the court as Stryker had been.

'They'll have their fancy lawyers all over the case. Even if we're in the right they'll stall and make us wait years for a judgement, and in the meantime Wingate'll have his claim ratified. Two years is nothing; look at how fast it went for us — for me, I mean.'

'Well, I just came to see you because I'll need a hand at the road ranch. There's a bunch of cattle coming through in two days' time, start of the trail season, and I'll need a few extra workers.'

'Don't worry; I'll be there. Right now I have a lot of feeding and cleaning to do, Merrill.' They gazed at each other, and he gave her a troubled smile.

'Abbey, let's not make this hard for ourselves.'

'We won't.' She stepped towards him and he longed to feel her in his arms as she had been in the early days when she first came to work with him. The pretence was the worst part of it all. He loved her as deeply as he had his first wife, but in the pursuit of land and some kind of future he had lost her, except for those times when he could be alone with her away from prying eyes. Out here that wasn't possible when the boys were around, and when Wingate or his men could arrive at any moment.

'I'll see you later,' she promised, and she wasn't just talking about work, he could see it in the sparkle in her eyes. He left her as a heartened man, while Abbey headed for the livery and the care of her animals.

★ ★ ★

Thorne decided that he was going to leave right away. He made sure that the few windows in the place were secure, and he barred the front door on the way out to make sure those bobcats that prowled around here, polecats, rats and other predators did not enter. They would regard a dead body as fresh meat to add to the larder. The old man had been a little scrawny, but that would not deter them.

He walked away from the ranch building cautiously, holding his Peacemakers as he looked around and listened for the slightest noise. Whoever had killed the old man might not take too kindly to the new owner of his spread. He reached his steed, stowed his guns away in his roomy pockets and rode off towards the town, over the undulating hills and through the low scrub that grew everywhere around here.

It was still early in the day and the town was busy, but people were going about their business peacefully enough. The sheriff's office was in Fuller Street, the main area of the town. The building had been constructed in the early settlement days, and as was the way of things had not been upgraded much since then. The lower half was made of redbrick and the upper of wood. It had a shuttered window to either side. The back of the office stuck out. This was where the cells were kept, and it was made of solid brick given the type of men who had to be housed there over the years.

'How do, Mr Thorne?' asked the

sheriff, who saved his visitor the trouble of entering by appealing at the faded blue door of the building.

'This is not a social visit,' said Thorne. 'I've just been up to the Bate homestead. Old Tom, he's dead.'

'The excitement of leaving to be with his son and family too much for his heart?' ventured Matt. 'Seen it happen before. I heard you were taking him to the railway station, seeing him off.'

'News travels fast in a town like this, but Tom isn't travelling anywhere, leastways not of his own volition. He's been shot dead, Sheriff.'

'Guess I'd better investigate then,' said Matt, not showing a great deal of emotion, even though this was a man he had known all his life.

'You don't seem that bothered.'

'Fact is, friend, violent death is the way of things out here.' He swallowed the last of his coffee, went inside and buckled on his gunbelt. 'Bud, you mind the fort while I'm gone.'

'I heard that, about Old Tom,' said

Bud. Unlike his superior he showed a degree of chagrin at the news. 'I hope you get whoever did this!'

'We'll see.' Matt strode out in the early day, and the two men were soon up in the hills and heading for the ranch. Thorne unlocked the front door.

'I see it didn't take you long to get the key,' said Matt.

'What do you mean by that?'

'So the story was true, you are taking over this place?'

'It's all settled, Sheriff, or it was until this happened.'

The sheriff inspected the body of the dead man.

'First thing I'd say is he knew who killed him.'

'What makes you think that?'

'Look around you, there's no sign of a violent struggle. Whoever did this came in, had a talk with the old feller, then pulled out a gun and plugged him straight in the heart. Tell me, Mr Thorne, what kind of guns you got?' As Thorne reached into his pocket to pull out one of his Peacemakers he noticed that the sheriff's hand hovered at his side, just above his own weapon. Thorne took out one of the weapons and laid it on the table.

'You got another the same?'

'Yep.' Thorne showed him. The sheriff inspected the weapons briefly.

'These ain't been fired recently, I can tell that much.'

'So I'm off the list of suspects?'

'I guess not; the murderer is often the person who discovers the body.' The sheriff walked around the building, and looked in the bedrooms and cooking area. 'Nothing, leastways nothing a killer might want, and it doesn't look as if anything's been taken. It's been a murder, pure and simple.' The two men left the building and the sheriff held out his hand after Thorne locked the door.

'What?'

'I want the keys. Right now this is a crime scene and the evidence is locked right there inside that building.'

'And what if I refuse?'

'It's just for a day or so until I ask a few questions around town, then you'll get them back. 'Sides, we won't be leaving Old Tom lying around there for long. The better weather's coming in and he won't last long.'

'That isn't going to happen.' Jubal shook his head and put the keys in his pocket. 'This is my property now. You just come to me when you need to get back in.'

'You do realize that makes it hard for me to trust you?'

'That might be the case, Sheriff, but I'm new to this area and I don't know whose pocket you're in.'

They rode back into town in grim silence. Thorne went to the sheriff's office, where he accounted for his actions that day and previous one.

'Well,' said Buck, 'I'll get Bud and we'll go around town, see if anyone has been up at the place. It's a remote chance, though, because it's a fair way out of town.'

The first place he went to was the

Wooden Barrel and the former gunman watched him leave. Thorne did not hesitate: he took what few worldly goods he had and returned to the Brewlins hotel where the owner met him in astonishment.

Lena appeared shortly afterwards when he had booked in for another day.

'What happened?' she asked.

'You came along at the right time,' he said. 'I needed a friendly face. It's Old Tom. I found him today and he's been murdered.'

'No!' Her face turned white.

'Whoever did this won't get away with it,' he said grimly. 'They're using him to send out a message to keep away. They don't know me very well if they think that's the case, and now I have a reason to stay; several reasons in fact if Abbey Watt comes into the picture.'

They were in the main hallway of the hotel and he heard a firm, womanly voice behind him.

'Are you taking my name in vain?'

Abbey had arrived.

13

The Wooden Barrel was filled with customers now that it was midday. Three barmen worked hard and as Matt Buck entered he could see some familiar faces in the busy interior. At the back were a couple of men playing cards with whom he wanted to speak.

Starry, the barman, looked pleased to see the sheriff.

'What can I get you, lawman?' he asked, holding up a beer glass and wiping it with a cloth.

'Maybe you can help me out,' said Matt. 'There's a problem that needs investigating and I think you might be able to do something for me.'

'Concerning what?'

'Concerning a murder.'

'Haven't heard a thing about any murders,' said Starry. 'Anyone I know?'

'Old Tom Bate.'

'Aww, the old guy. He was going to leave, be with his family back east.'

'Well he's going nowhere now, 'cept six feet down.'

'Who did it?'

'Well that's what I don't rightly know, so if you could keep your ears open for me I'd be obliged.'

'I'll do that,' said Starry, his mouth a thin, firm line. He had liked Old Tom, who on auction days had been a good customer who had generously paid for drinks for all his friends. Tom had been funny too, often regaling them with stories from his colourful past and his many encounters with the natives, most of which had been life threatening in one way or another.

Matt went over to the familiar faces and he lifted his chin at the three men who sat there, indicating that he wanted to speak to them.

'Outside,' he said. Once out in the heat of day, but with a chill breeze that blew at their backs, he faced up to Wingate, Venters and Lewis, all of

130

whom were armed.

'Where have you boys been all day?' he asked.

'Finished off a bit of fencing on my new claim,' said Wingate, 'then came out here for a drink or two and a harmless game of cards.'

'So you were nowhere near the Bate ranch?'

'See, Sheriff, we're working men,' said Lewis, 'we don't have time to mess around this area.'

'From what I see you have plenty of time to drink and play at cards.'

'Don't rightly know what you're saying,' said Wingate. 'Any reason why we should be talking about the Bate spread?'

'Maybe you can tell me.' He looked at their somewhat weatherworn faces. Wingate gave a sudden, satisfied nod.

'He's dead, ain't he? Old Tom I mean.'

'Now, would you just happen to have some special knowledge that would tell you that was the case, Dabs, or did you just take a wild guess?'

'Wasn't so wild, Sheriff, given you were asking Starry some pretty pointed questions, then you come over to us and start asking us things about where we were today.'

'Sheriff, why are you interrogating my men?'

The four of them had been standing at the edge of the boardwalk, with Buck facing the other three, horse traffic going up and down the street beside them. Now, as Matt turned he could see that one of the animals had halted behind him. He turned and had to squint upwards, since the sun was behind the man on the large brown gelding. He was seated in a big, comfortable Western saddle, the kind a man could sit on for days when he was riding the trail.

'Well, Mr Stryker, way I see it there are a few questions that need answering, and if you're the law around here and you need to find something out, you ask.'

'These here boys were on a bona fide mission for me today, Sheriff. Guess that kind of lets them off the hook.' Stryker dismounted heavily from his horse. The sun showed the wisps of white hair that stuck out from under his hat. He moved a little stiffly now as if he had been exerting himself already that day. For the first time the sheriff began to think of Stryker as being old. He had known Stryker for twenty years, knew him for the ruthless cattleman he was, and also knew that his men would follow him to the end; he engendered a kind of loyalty that had more to do with his powerful personality than just having him as a boss.

The way the old cattle trader had taken away the first love of his life with his money and his experience of life still rankled, but Matt told himself that this didn't matter, that he had to remain aloof and not let such things colour his thinking.

'He says we might have murdered Old Tom,' said Wingate. 'We didn't touch him, none of us.'

'What? One of my fellow ranchers has been murdered?' asked Stryker. 'This is terrible news. He was just going to leave his ranch too.'

'You sure seem to know a great deal about his business,' said the sheriff.

'Well, yes, I would do, Sheriff. You see, he had agreed to let me have the land. It would be useful for my own operations in that area. Isn't that right, Dabs?'

'In principle he had agreed,' said Wingate.

'That can't be right,' said the sheriff. 'I was with the man who reported the murder, and he's just told me he bought the whole lot from Tom the other day.'

'Who would that be?'

'Guess I don't want to give too much away, Mr Stryker, not while I'm still investigating this case.'

'I think you've been seeing Jubal Thorne, and I also think you know who the murderer is. You see, Thorne doesn't own that land any more than you do.'

'Is there an undertaker in town?' asked Thorne.

'There's Julias Frankel. He's behind the main street,' said Abbey. 'What's going on here?'

'There's been a murder,' said Jubal, then he explained his discovery to her briefly. 'The sheriffs already been up there. He's seen enough. I'm going to make sure that the old man is buried in his own property, where he spent the best years of his life.'

'Tom?' Her hand flew to her mouth. 'This is terrible; do you know who did it?'

'No, I don't, but I do know that all his cattle are gone, so you must have sent your boys to fetch them.'

'Leave her alone,' said Lena, 'Abbey's never raised a hand in violence in her life.'

'There's always a first time,' said Thorne.

'My boys were unarmed,' she said.

'Besides which, what would have been the point of killing Tom, even if we had been that kind of people? He had already given us what we wanted.' Her eyes were distinctly blurred now although she did not shed any tears. Self-control was a big part of who she was.

'Then I'm going to make sure it's all settled,' said Jubal. 'We'll get Tom buried and I'll take possession of my new property.'

'Doesn't it bother you?'

'What bothers me is that someone thinks they're going to scare me away from what is mine,' said Thorne grimly. 'I'll dig the old man's grave with my own hands if need be, but I won't leave just because someone wants me to go.'

'Lena, I'm sorry. I was in town to chase up that seed order and thought I would come and see you and talk over old times, but this is worse than I thought.'

'Don't worry,' said Lena tightly. 'Just know that you have a lot more friends in this town than you think.'

'Thanks, I mean it.' For a moment the two women smiled at each other, one tall and commanding, the other shorter, softer and much more feminine.

'I'll show you where the funeral parlour is,' said Abbey, leaving with Thorne and walking across town. She came in with him while Thorne made the arrangements for the funeral, and she was with him as they rode back to Thorne's ranch. This time Julias Frankel — a short, dark, unsmiling man — and his two husky assistants accompanied them. They did not bring the funeral carriage that he used in town, but instead used a buckboard with a simple pine coffin loaded on to the back.

Jubal took Frankel to a corner of the land facing Coltsfoot Pass through which travellers had to come to get to the ranch.

'Would you be able to bury him here?' The undertaker agreed and, while the two young men set to work with broad D-shaped shovels, Thorne went to the ranch with Abbey, Lena, whom they had picked up on the way, and Frankel. The two women were shocked, but they prepared Tom with respect and reverence, scooting the men out while they dressed him in his Sunday best, a suit that had not been worn for a long time. Then, with the help of the men, they put him in his coffin, the lid of which was nailed down by Frankel, and took him on the buckboard to his final resting place.

Thorne assisted the men to lower the coffin into the grave, and then he said a short oration over the grave, giving the 'ashes to ashes' speech in a quiet but powerful manner, with an assurance that affected all there, before picking up a handful of dirt and rattling it down atop the unvarnished pine coffin. The others did the same, and then the two young men made short work of filling in the grave. Both women had eyes that were red from weeping.

Jubal paid the undertaker, and gave a good tip to his two young assistants. There was a look about him that Abbey had never seen before. It was the look of a man who was breathing in and holding his breath before letting it back out again, a man who was holding back. She didn't know what that feeling was in the air around him, just that she felt scared and reassured at the same time.

He let the funeral director and his workers leave and he looked at the two women.

'If his son wants to take him back out east I'll arrange for that to happen. Until then, at least this way he's at rest. Come on, I'll get you into town.'

He rode in front of them and the two women followed, Lena on her mare and Abbey on her gelding. Although they rode well enough, they were hardly able to keep up with him and his big black horse, although he waited patiently enough for them at times. Finally they stood together in the middle of town beside their horses.

'I have to go back to the hotel,' said Lena. 'I had to arrange to come with you at the last minute as it was. Thank you, Mr Thorne.'

'Jubal, and you did Old Tom proud,' he said, smiling faintly for first time that day. She left, feeling somehow glad that he had been there with him, despite the terrible events of the day.

'I guess I'd best be getting back to my work too,' said Abbey. 'It's not fair leaving the boys with everything.'

'I guess not.' He looked at her steadily. 'You asked for my help a few days ago, didn't you?'

'Things change mighty fast around here.'

'I guess we both know who did this, or at least who got one of their men to do this.'

'Do we have to say it out loud?'

'If someone strikes out at me, do you know what I do, Abbey?'

She looked steadily into his face, his low almost hypnotic voice drawing her attention. 'What do you do, Mr Thorne?'

'Why,' he said, 'I strike back twice as hard. Now, I guess you have something to show me.'

14

The sheriff stepped back.

'What are you trying to tell me?' asked Matt.

'Well, Sheriff, look at it this way.' Stryker paused and narrowed his eyes. He was standing closer to the sheriff than his men and Matt could feel the sheer power of the man. 'Sometimes you've got to look facts in the face. This Thorne, or whatever he's called, appears out of nowhere just at the right moment.'

'I don't know what you mean by that.'

'Things are never that easy,' said Stryker, 'so he turns up just at the time when there's a ranch for sale and he wants to grab a bit of land. A bit too convenient that, wouldn't you say, son?'

'I don't like being called 'son' for a start,' said Matt. 'You don't get by patronising me, Stryker.'

'That's Mr Stryker to you,' interrupted Wingate, starting forward a little, but halted by the big landowner holding up his hand.

'Easy there, Dabs. No use antagonising the law. The man here's just doing his job. So, what was I talking about again?'

Matt was not fooled by this old man act; he knew that Stryker was controlling every word that issued from his lips.

'Yep, that's what I was saying. This here Thorne — appropriate name because he's like a thorn in our sides at the moment — he turns up and claims that there's land for sale and the old man sold it to him.'

'I don't know what you're trying to say.'

'Old Tom there, he was a neighbour; I was young when I started out here and he was already in his middle years. I guess what I'm saying is that news like that shakes us all up.'

'Why would that be, Mr Stryker?'

142

'When you lose someone you've known that well for that long, it seems to me that someone needs to pay for what they've done.'

'I'll tell you right now: Thorne found the body when he went up to take the old man away to town and get him on the next train.'

'So he says.'

'Now look here, Stryker, you better have a direct accusation or I'm walking away from here, and you'll all remain suspects.'

'I went to see Tom and he as good as said I was getting the ranch,' said Stryker. 'Ain't that right, Dabs?'

'Certainly seemed that way,' said Wingate, cool and watchful. The sheriff looked at the two men. He noticed that Lewis and Venters had pulled away and were looking at the ground, keeping out of the way.

'He was stalling,' said Stryker. 'Wanted a better price so that he could retire with a good backing behind him and didn't want to be a burden to his son. It's all business so I told him I would think about it.'

This was true in one respect: Matt knew that Stryker was a hard business-man, and would dicker for every penny that he spent. It would hardly have been a surprise to him that he would not have settled on a deal right away.

'Then this Thorne came in, said he had bought the land and the ranch, out of nowhere, and it's all settled.'

'So why would he kill the old man?'

'Well, I heard from Tom when he was in town the other day that he didn't want to sell that land and that he was still discussing the whole matter with Thorne. He didn't want to deal with a stranger, but it's even worse than that.'

'What do you mean?'

'Funny how he went there with that old boiled hen, Abbey Watt.'

'Now don't talk about her that way,' said the sheriff. 'She has a lot of friends in this town.'

'She's stepped on a lot of toes,' said Stryker, 'and she's not doing it for herself; it all goes back to Merrill Avery.' He looked at the sheriff with hooded eyes. 'They're living a lie and you know these things as well as I do. They're breaking the very act that was enacted by the government to help settlers.'

'You mean that ranch ain't really hers?'

'Exactly, it's his as much as the trail eatery and you know it too.'

'I think I know what you're saying.'

'So the old boiler needs a brand. She hires herself a bounty hunter who decides he wants a change of pace, and he'll help her out for a goodly sum of money. Merrill's got the funds, he's making a fortune with his eatery.'

'For Jesus' sake,' said Matt, 'it was Thorne who discovered the body. Why would he shoot a man and alert me to the fact? It don't make sense.'

'Double bluff,' said Stryker, 'and he's played you with it. He's a murderer all right; we've heard stories about him. He's a brazenfaced liar and he killed the old man because Tom didn't want him to have the ranch. He told you because he knows that there would soon be a fuss when he set up shop and the old man was never seen again. Tom's son would have cottoned on sooner than later.'

'But the deeds would've been ratified with a lawyer.'

'What lawyer? When you catch up with Thorne, ask him. Then find the lawyer. I tell you, the man's a liar and a killer. Just you watch, he'll do something that shows he's in with Abbey Watt, and then you'll need to arrest him for the good of us all.'

'I'll keep it in mind,' said Matt, turning away from the small group of men and looking directly at their employer. 'You're a clever man, Stryker, but that don't mean might is right. Thorne may be what you say, but on the other hand he might be completely innocent.'

'Right, men, get back to work,' said Stryker. 'The sheriff's finished here, ain't you Matt?'

'There'll be further questions,' said the sheriff.

'You've got your man already,' said Stryker getting back on his gelding. 'You'll see.' He rode off down the street, a big confident man, his workers taking off on the opposite direction. Matt Buck walked on, a sorely troubled man.

⋆ ⋆ ⋆

Thorne rode with Abbey out to her ranch. He could see why this was a place where she would have wanted to settle. The landscape beyond Clearwater Valley was not promising in terms of feed for cattle, consisting of rolling hills, undulating plains and low scrubland. The grass that grew in areas outside the valley tended to be tougher and harder for the animals to crop. Down here in the valley there was one thing that the larger areas of land did not have, and that was irrigation. The

Clearwater River was not particularly huge, especially during the summer when the winter rains dried up, but it was big enough to leech into the surrounding landscape. This, along with rich soils that washed down from hills, meant that the surrounding parts were green and lush.

'What I don't understand,' said Thorne as they arrived at the valley, 'is why the cattle barons haven't tried to annex this area before.'

'Then you don't know the history of Clearwater,' said Abbey. Thorne noted that the lines of worry that had been etched across her face since earlier that day had faded as they arrived back at the place that she called home. 'You see, although the land spreads out here, if you look across the other side of the valley there's only a narrow strip of land beside the water.'

'Yep, I guess that's because of the way the landscape slopes down from the Carbon Hills and creates a flood-plain in this area in the bad weather.

Over thousands of years that forward motion has created the shape of the valley as it is today.'

'Why, Mr Thorne,' she gave him a sideways, admiring glance as they followed the road down to the eatery, 'you're beginning to make me think you're an educated man.'

'I try my best not to give that impression,' he said. 'Puts people on edge if they think you're giving yourself airs and graces, and I haven't had a chance to wear either of those in recent years.'

'Maybe it's time you settled down.'

'That was kind of the intention.'

★　★　★

They came to the eatery. Merrill Avery employed a number of local people, mostly female, and he liked to keep an eye on his workers and serve in his own premises. It was not long before they were able to get hold of him. He expressed some surprise at the presence of the former bounty hunter, but agreed readily enough to accompany the pair of them to her ranch. Thorne could see by his expression that he wanted to ask them many questions but Avery, who was a taciturn man, could sense an air of urgency from them and the simplest way was to follow in their course.

'Guess I never answered your question about them cattle barons,' said Abbey. 'See, in the better weather this trail has always been open to those bringing their cattle down from other states: it's part of the Oregon trail and it means quicker, easier progress for the herders.'

'So the land was always being used, and therefore stock could not be brought here for mere feeding purposes, and as it was always common land the CTA wouldn't want to interfere with those who were their trading partners.'

'You really do catch on mighty quick.' He could hear the growing admiration in her voice.

'Now things have changed with this Homesteading Act and they're seeing themselves as under threat.'

'The worst of it,' said Merrill, 'is that they're probably right.'

By this time they had arrived at her ranch, which was set back from the Oregon Trail on land that was framed by the Clearwater River and the trail on one side and by the high hills of the valley on the other. He could see that she and her companions had been working hard here, and that this was a nice little operation, one that could be profitable for someone who built up their stock and had some sort of ambition. They got off their horses and led them to her livery. There they unsaddled their horses, led them into the cool of the building and made sure they had feed and water.

'Time for some food,' she said, and they headed to the ranch. A second floor had been added, and the way the ranch was kept told him that this was a woman who knew what she was doing. It was not a fancy spread by any means but, again, it had the makings of a good home, and she had done all this in two years, albeit with a great deal of help.

They had a simple meal of bread, corn, bacon and eggs, followed by cups of coffee, and spoke little of the reason why he was here, but at the end of the meal Avery took issue with their visitor, aghast as he was at the news of what had happened to Tom.

'Thorne, you don't strike me as a man who does much in the way of paying social visits.'

'You do me an injustice,' said Thorne. 'Guess I just wanted to see what Abbey was up against, and saying that I also guess it's time for me to go a little walk.' He went out of the ranch building and simply walked around the ranch.

'You didn't finish what you were saying about how things have changed around here,' he said.

'The cattle trails are being used less and less because of the coming of the railways,' said Abbey as they walked towards the end of her property. 'That was why I was able to file my claim, and it's also why Stryker is moving in on me.'

Thorne was now able to see it with his own eye. There in the middle of the green grass was a cabin that looked as if it would blow away in a strong wind. Barely the size of a horsebox, it was clear that this was no human habitation. Then there was the fencing; it stretched all the way from Abbey's boundaries, hard up against her own, taking in a huge expanse of the green sward, and in effect cutting off her animals from easy sustenance.

'Well,' said Thorne, 'let's see how we can take this down.'

15

Matt Buck was not finished yet. He went to see one of the only two law firms in town — Gabbatis and Flynn — only to find that no one there knew what he was talking about. That left him to go and see Justin Burrows. The only problem being that there was no sign of the lawyer, the offices locked and empty as he discovered when he peered in the front window. There could have been someone working away at the back of the building but the place had an air of neglect that spoke of it being empty for a few days. Not being a particularly trusting man, he decided to investigate a little more and went into the hardware store beside the lawyer's office. The store sold everything from candles to guns, with a good selection of Colts, Winchesters and Smith & Wessons on sale, not all of them brand

154

new, and the ammunition to go with them.

The owner, a big man called Gruber, with a pretty daughter called Amy who was also serving in the shop, was quite vocal.

'I know nothing; the man is not being here that is all. One day he is here and the next gone.'

'But didn't he have an office boy?'

'*O Ja*, I suppose. That boy, he comes in here sometimes.' The owner took a sideways look at his daughter. 'But they are now gone.'

'Well, thank you for your help,' said the sheriff, but Gruber merely grunted and turned back to his stocktaking. The sheriff gave a nod to the pretty girl and headed for the door. He was out on the boardwalk, with the door just creaking shut behind, when a quicksilver shape darted in front of him.

'Wait, Sheriff, I just told Pa I needed a breath of fresh air.'

'How are you, Amy?'

'I saw what happened. You see, Pa

likes a glass or two of rotgut at night and he ain't so sharp at getting up early, but that's a time when we get a lot of business. I was here when they came for him.'

'Came for him? Bowers you mean? Did someone drag him away?'

'No, it wasn't like that at all; two big men came along in a hired carriage. I was unbolting the door and pulling the shutters open at the time and I guess I was in shadow. Anyway, Justin — he had a quiet chat with them, said something about fetching his office boy, got in the carriage and they all rumbled off.'

'So did you hear who they were?'

'Yes, they were from the railway, said they wanted him to do some contract work worth big money, but he had to travel out south that day.'

'Amy, thanks a lot. You've helped me out.'

'That's all light, Sheriff,' she gave him a winning smile, 'and it wasn't his office boy I was interested in. I hope

Justin comes back soon.' She blushed in a becoming manner and hurried back into the store. Looking after her, the sheriff thought that Justin Bowers was a very lucky man.

He went straight to the telegraph office and sent a wire off to the railway company asking them to get Justin Bowers in touch with him at once because Tom Bate was dead. He could see why the young man would have jumped at a chance like this, but it also left the sheriff in a quandary. He did not know yet if Jubal Thorne was simply who he said he was, or was in some scheme to rob and kill innocent people as Stryker had said.

He headed for the saloon in the company of his deputy. It was where they would learn what was going on, if anywhere.

* * *

'What weapons do you have?' said Jubal Thorne to his companions.

'I have my shotgun,' said Abbey

promptly, 'that's all, really, aside from plenty of sharp knives, clubs and sticks.'

'And you?' He turned to Merrill.

'I have quite a few, since things have been rough at odd times,' said Merrill. 'Some handguns, a couple of Winchesters and plenty of ammo.' He looked at Thorne with some degree of alarm.

'You ain't thinking of attacking his men or cattle are you?'

'We wouldn't put up with that,' said Abbey firmly. 'We don't need those kinds of complications. I have one pistol, that does me.'

'I'm real sure of that,' said Thorne, 'but you just make sure that Miss Watt here has a few weapons, and get those boys armed, because we're lifting that fencing and we're doing it right now.' They both looked at him as if he had gone completely mad. 'I'll explain why. They haven't brought down any animals yet, because it's the start of the season. Once the cows are here it could get real messy. If you want to stop them we have to do it now.'

'I see the sense in what you're saying,' agreed Abbey.

'Well I don't . . . Have the two . . . ' Avery fought for breath like a man who had just been running. 'Have the two of you gone just plain loco?' he asked.

'Really?' She looked him straight in the eye. 'This is my ranch and I'll do what I want around here. I ain't the type to keep cowering away from what has to be done. Come with me, Jubal.'

As he followed her to the livery, Thorne caught the look on Merrill Avery's face. It was the look of a man who had opened Pandora's box and released a hellish entity he had not known existed.

The two young men were made available. They had plenty of work to do around the ranch, but they were neglecting their normal duties to help out the strange visitor. For once Abbey held back as Jubal spoke to them.

'They've annexed the land, and they've left to roister, get drunk and chase a woman or two, which is good for us. Now we're going to do what needs to be done. I'll need rope, harnesses and the strongest horses you've got.' This was when Abbey went into the livery and triumphantly led out the largest horse that Jubal had ever seen. 'That one might do,' he said, in an understated tone that somehow made her smile despite the seriousness of the situation. 'We'll get a yoke on his shoulders, attach a strong rope and get to work. We'll do the same with other horses. I'll take this one and show you what to do.'

Once the rope was attached he led the big animal to the part of the new fence nearest to the ranch. He tied the other end of the rope to the horizontal crossbar of the fence, then took the horse's harness and led the big creature forward. The job was not quite as hard as it looked because the upright posts of the fence had been battered into the ground using sledgehammers, without mortar to fix them into the ground. A section of fence about six feet long pulled away. It was tied to the other sections with wire, but Abbey had a good pair of pliers and she used these to snip the wire ties, and suddenly there was a section of the fence lying on the green sward in front of them.

'You guys, you'll start at the other end with one of the other horses,' said Jubal. 'Abbey there'll have the task of separating the sections, and you two will have the task of stacking the fencing beside that makeshift piece of junk in the middle of the meadow.' He meant that uninhabitable shack that passed for Wingate's ranch.

'I say we chuck 'em in the river, said Billy, let 'em drown trying to get 'em back.'

'Would serve them right,' said Cyrus, 'what do you think, Mr Thorne?'

'Boys, I know how much fun that would be, said Jubal, and I would do that in a minute if I thought it would do us any good, but you just get on with the job and stack the fencing in the middle, like I asked you to do, and we'll get on fine.'

Having said this, he got to work

immediately, tying the ropes on and having the massive animal pull the sections of fencing out one by one.

It was hard, monotonous work because there was so much of the new fencing and there was no way they could have done the job without the help of the two young men, who started at the opposite end and worked their way towards him. The fact was, though, that because it had taken much wielding of sledgehammers to knock in the stakes used for the fencing, it was much easier to pull out a section of fencing than it had been to put it in.

With Abbey helping to cut the wires that bound the sections together, and the boys pulling them into the middle beside the makeshift ranch, it wasn't long before the pile began to grow.

It was tiring work, but Jubal did not let them let up with the process because he knew only too well that they were up against time. It would not be long before the arrival of those who would challenge what they were doing.

162

'Where's Merrill?' he asked at one point as he continued leading the big horse forward.

'He's away to get those weapons you were talking about,' said Abbey. 'You don't think we've put ourselves into a lot of danger, do you?' He stopped leading the big animal for a moment and looked at her seriously.

'You're standing up for your rights by taking back something that's not just yours, but belongs to everyone in Brewlins: the right to grazing.'

'Stryker would say I'm stealing this ranch from another homesteader. The one I've built, I mean.'

'In what way?'

'Well, he would say it's really Merrill's land, that I'm just doing what I was told, that it's really three-hundred-and-twenty acres including the trail eatery, all his.'

'And what would your answer be to that?'

'Let's get this fencing down,' she answered, and that was all he needed.

The two young men did sterling work at their end, pulling down the wood to the side of the meadow, pulling it to the middle, with never a complaint even though they sweated mightily as they went about their task.

Jubal stopped, finally, and looked at what they had done. In one afternoon a woman, two husky young men, and wispy gunslinger — with the aid of a particularly fine draught animal — had undone days and even weeks of work performed by Stryker's men.

Avery had come back by this time, and when he saw what they had done he shook his head and turned pale.

'This sure is going to mean war,' he said.

'Time for you all to go inside,' said Thorne. 'We'll face up to what they're going to do when they arrive.'

Abbey began to prepare a meal of boiled ham, potatoes and corn, ably assisted by Avery, who was an expert by now in the quick preparation of food. They sat around the table in the early evening light that filtered though the twin windows of the ranch, and after Abbey said grace they had their meal. They were all exhausted, and the animals still had to be tended too, but they were all conscious of a job well done.

Despite the danger that lurked in their collective decision.

16

As in the Bible, those who had constructed the fence had been allowed their day of rest. They had roistered at the local saloons celebrating a real achievement. Many hours of annoying sweaty work had gone into closing off what had once been common land.

Wingate, Lewis and Venters had been sent to look over their handiwork. They had been keeping a close eye on the fenced-off meadows; now they were going down to make sure the preparations were in place for the following day. This was when Stryker was moving in his animals to feed and support Wingate's claim. They all knew that once the animals were there it would be hard for Watt and her friends to get them out. The reason they were worried about damage was because she might have been the one most visibly affected, but other smallholders in the area had objected to what was happening too and might want to make their mark. As they rode towards Abbey's spread, Stryker's men saw that the fencing was gone. All of it, not just one or two sections.

'Well I'll be cussed in the entire world,' said Wingate, getting off his horse and leading him to the spot where the gates should have been. 'What the hell has gone down here?'

'It's that Abbey Watt,' said Lewis, 'she did this.'

'I'm inclined to believe you, Jim,' said Wingate, 'but she must have had some kind of help.'

It was early evening now, and the men could smell the smoke from wood-burning stoves drifting in the air, and caught the scent of the green, juicy grass that their beeves should have been consuming the following day. Wingate fought not to get into a blind rage, but he was looking at weeks of hard work destroyed in one day. Not just the actual fence work, but the buying and constructing of materials and the planning put into the event.

With his two men flanking him he walked in an uptight fashion along the road to Abbey's ranch. With a gesture that made his companions step back he pulled out his gun and fired three shots into the air. In the countryside around them, hemmed in by the hills of the valley, the pistol shots sounded like explosions of cannon.

'Come out, you bitch,' said Wingate. 'Explain yourself, you thieving witch.'

The door opened and a man appeared whom they all recognized. The new owner of the Bate spread. He was in his long coat, a breeze flapping the dusty hem against his stout boots, his long, coppery hair half-covering his face. He was hatless, his hands hovering over his pockets.

'Do you gentlemen have a problem?' he asked in conversational tones.

'We're here to see that thieving tramp, Abbey Watt,' said Wingate.

'Well, she isn't at home to you,' said Thorne. 'I suggest you go on your way peacefully.'

'She's gone and jumped my claim,' said Wingate, 'stolen all my fencing.'

'That fencing wasn't yours,' said Thorne. 'Secondly, Abbey never stole a thing. You go to your pretend shack and you'll find not one bit of your wood, wire, or anything else has been taken. It's all there, every single scrap, which brings me to my next point. Take it away as soon as you can. The other homesteaders stood by, worried about what might happen to them. Well, I'm telling them what will happen. Those meadows will remain common land.' By this time Thorne had stepped off the porch and he was facing them.

Wingate, gun still in hand, stepped forward. Lewis and Venters hovered their own hands above their holsters.

'You gonna tell her, and whoever helped her do this, to restore that fencing,' said Wingate tightly, 'or there'll be real trouble.'

'Go away right now,' said Thorne.

'There's already a court petition in to say that's common land, and if you're the petitioner who wants to show his claim as legit, you'll be there.'

'You're bluffing,' said Wingate, but his narrow face was blushing red with anger. He lifted his gun slightly, but even before he could get in a position to let the weapon speak for him, an event occurred that nonplussed him and those he was with. The lone man swept the coppery locks away from the side of his face revealing his visage as it really was. The dark green eye patch had been pulled up to his hair in anticipation of this encounter.

This was a face like no other they had seen. He had a skeletal aspect to the left side of the skull where the flesh had been melted and puckered by some catastrophic event in his past. Worst of all was the left eye, where the flesh had become tight and the eye stared out from a hollow, skeletal cavity. The grinning mask on that side of his face overpowered the rest and suddenly they seemed to be looking at a demon straight from hell.

Venters even made the sign of the cross, reverting back to the religion of his youth.

Worse still, the demon had a Peacemaker in either hand, the worn handles showing that the weapons were not for mere decoration.

'Now, I suggest you three get out of here,' said Thorne. 'Tell your master that he's finished with his little take-over, or the folks around here'll have a lot to say about it.'

'The hell with it.' Wingate could not look a coward in front of his compatri-ots. The lone gunman knew this and gave him a way out. He lowered his Peacemakers.

'I'll let you see sense and get out of here; this is just a friendly chat.'

Wingate had been given a way out. He holstered his gun.

'All right, we're leaving. No point sticking around when the deed is done; but this ain't finished, not by a long way.' He spat on the ground and made a great show of striding off with his men. As they rode off, they all knew, including the man in the shadows who stood and watched them go, that this was far from over.

★　★　★

Stryker was not the kind of man who took bad news on the chin. It was Wingate who went to his home and told their boss what had happened with the fencing. At first Stryker had been incredulous.

'All of it?' he asked referring to the fact that the fencing had been taken and stacked near the so-called 'ranch' that seemed to belong to Wingate, even though its real ownership was an open secret.

'Every last one of them,' said Wingate soberly. He gave an involuntary shudder. 'You just don't know what it was like, not the fencing, but him. He put the scares up every last man-jack who was there.'

'I'll kill that son-of-whore,' said Stryker, 'I'll do it with my own hands. You . . . you were useless. He was threatening the three of you; you could have gunned down the dog and borne witness for each other.'

'It wasn't that simple,' said Wingate. 'Merrill Avery might have been there; certainly that there woman and her two boys were watching.' He was disturbed by the fact that the big man, who stood outside his own home, was buzzing with anger. He looked as if he was going to jump on his huge gelding and ride out there on his own to complete the deed. The trouble with such an idea, besides not knowing what conditions he would be facing when he got there, was that it was now evening and the light was fading fast as it did around these parts. A younger Stryker would not have hesitated under these conditions to leave for the valley and use whatever weaponry he had to hand. It was said that he had many a confrontation of this type when he was building up his business. And anger, it seemed, was still the spur for his actions.

'No, wait,' he said rubbing his chin. 'I have to think this through. He doesn't belong there, and he has his ranch. I don't think he's going to be there this night. He'll crawl back to his rat-hole and swelter there like the dog he is. I know exactly what to do. We've got to tackle this thing in two ways. Wingate, get to your bed real soon, but not before you get to the bunkhouse and speak to the other men.'

'Why?'

'Because what I'm going to do will involve all of us getting up well before dawn. Now, come to think of it, before you give your little speech we have to go to the sheriff.'

'Why's that, boss?'

'Because we're going to set Sheriff Buck onto a killer — and get him out of the way at the same time.'

★ ★ ★

Jubal Thorne waited until the men were out of sight and then addressed Abbey, Merrill and the two young men.

'If you keep your heads down this will blow over. I can promise you right away that nothing will happen while this landowner friend of yours considers his options.'

'But what if he sends someone out tonight?' Avery spoke in a tone of despair, his features ashen in the light of the oil lamps that Abbey used to illuminate her home.

Jubal had covered his face again, lifting his eye patch down, and he'd had his back to them the whole time he had been confronting the men, so they did not know the full extent of his warning.

'I got to go back to my new spread. It's close to Stryker's ranch; I wouldn't put it past him to torch the place in revenge, sending out a couple of his lowlife worms to do so. Tomorrow I'm going into town to get some stock. As far as I'm concerned it is business as usual.' At the door, he turned to Abbey.

'Oh, and you'd better meet me in town because I'm going to take out a deposition against Wingate and therefore Stryker. I'd rather go by the law on this one. Once there's some sort of judgement against him, Wingate will no longer have a claim and they'll have to take that damn fencing away completely.'

'He might fight the case,' said Abbey, 'but then again he'll have to prove that Wingate is setting up on his own, and why would he be letting a cattleman of that size take over the common grazing? I think you might be right.'

'I'll see you later,' said Jubal, putting on his wide brimmed hat. He thanked Cyrus and Billy for their hard work, and promised them a hard cash reward after he had been to the bank, giving them an eagle each as an award for now.

'Don't forget, Cy, you're doing those irrigation ditches beside the eatery tomorrow,' said Avery. 'The work there can't stop.'

'Sure,' said Cyrus, not looking too

pleased at the thought, but it was those very ditches that kept the fields just beyond Avery's ranch lush enough for the trail men to feed cattle.

'Why are you helping us?' asked Abbey, following Thorne out.

'As I said, if someone strikes at you, you hit them back twice as hard,' said Jubal. 'And remember to give that big horse of yours extra oats as a reward. He was a trooper today.' He tipped his hat to her, got on Eb and rode quickly towards his new home. It was a long, lonely ride up to the ranch, but he valued the time involved because it gave him a chance to think about what he was doing. The removal of the fencing had been a dramatic gesture — not to mention one that had left him with an aching back and legs — but it should show Stryker that he meant business.

The kind of business he meant by this was not that of taking anything away or engaging in some kind of battle: it was real business, the hard economics of what they were doing out here. Stryker would pay for the death of the old man — but that would come later. Thorne just wanted to establish that he would not be treated with contempt in such a casual fashion. These big landowners were soft and slow to respond; Thorne was certain in his own mind as he reached the empty spread that it would take Stryker a few days to regroup, and by that time Thorne would have visited a few other smallholders, got a petition with their support, and the deposition would have been filed.

As he lit the lamps, saw to his horse and then retired to bed to rest his aching frame, Thorne was pleased with this days work. He had given himself time.

If only he could have seen one day ahead.

17

Sheriff Matt Buck was in his office, even at ten o'clock that night. He was drinking a java with Bud when he heard the thumping on the door. The building was all in one piece because his living quarters were next door, and as comfortable as a single man could make them. He had been preparing to discuss the case of the newcomer and the dead man with Bud when the banging alerted them both. It was not unusual to be disturbed even in the middle of the night, particularly at weekends when the saloons were full to bursting with cattlemen and miners. He could pretty much expect to jail at least one or two hotheads, but this was the start of the week and he was usually left alone at this time.

He opened the door to find Stryker, Wingate and Lewis all standing there. Stryker did not hang around, but simply came into the building with the air of a man who was used to getting his own way. Bud scrambled to his feet and limped back towards the shadowy area where the cells were, keeping a wary eye on the new visitors.

'To what do I owe the pleasure?' asked Matt.

'Sheriff, much as the men here enjoy your company, this ain't a social visit,' said Stryker. 'Ain't that right fellas?' They nodded dutifully. 'Well, let's get down to business. These men were attacked when they went out to check on a lawful claim. Tell the sheriff, Dabs,' said Stryker.

Wingate related the tale of how he had gone to check out his land, preparatory to bringing down some stock, only to find that his fencing had gone, and then he and his men were menaced by a lone gunman who was prepared to shoot them dead if they got in his way.

'So you're filing a complaint?' asked Matt.

'We sure are,' said Wingate. 'This man is dangerous, and as I said before,

180

he's in league with that tough gal Abbey Watt. There's a conspiracy between them two, I can tell you, else why would he be there threatening respectable citizens?'

'And you're a witness?' the sheriff was speaking to Lewis.

'I sure am,' said that stalwart. 'Why, I was feared he was going to blow my head clean off a my shoulders.'

'And were you there too?' asked Matt of Stryker.

'No, sir, I was busy managing my own land and my own business, but I just wanted to help these fine upstanding citizens — men, I may say, who have given this town a lot of trade over the years. Now Wingate, moving to his own settlement, has been treated like this.' Stryker's voice was suitably indignant at the maltreatment of his friend.

'The impression I got of the miscreant was that he was ready to go to his own place,' said Wingate.

'That's right, his big black hoss was hitched right at the side of the building,' said Lewis.

'So you think he'll be back at Tom's — I mean his new spread?' asked Matt.

'I surely do,' said Wingate. 'You got to put a stop to this, Sheriff. One man can cause real trouble for a whole community if he goes about things like this, and we all know he must've murdered Old Tom.'

'There's still no proof of that,' snapped the sheriff.

'At the end of it all, I guess we need to know what you intend to do,' said Stryker. 'The members of the CTA pay good money in taxes to this county. We want to know that a man can go about his legitimate business without being molested in this way.'

'And what about you, Stryker, what are you getting out of it?'

'Whoah, Sheriff. Just being a good citizen.'

'Tomorrow I'll go up and see to Mr Thorne. I'll bring him in for questioning and I guess your men can file charges if they so wish.'

'Well, if I were you I'd be up there at

first light. He strikes me as an early riser,' said Stryker. 'Guess that's about it. Thank you for your time. Thanks to you, Bud, for keeping an eye on things.' The men departed, but as they did so Matt could see a twisted smile on the face of Lewis that he did not like.

'What do you think?' he asked sitting down and drinking some of his now cold coffee, which tasted like ashes in his mouth.

'I think they were telling some of the truth,' said Bud. 'I don't think it's the whole story by a long chalk.'

'Guess it's time to bring him in, meaning Thorne, but it's pitch black out there. You go home to your missus, Bud, and I'll get settled here,' said Matt.

'I'll see you first thing, then,' said Bud. He put down his own coffee and moved steadily towards the door, his limp more pronounced due to being tired.

Matt stared at the untidy surface of his desk for a long time. Instinctively he liked Jubal Thorne and Abbey Watt, but the law was the law and he was going to have to enforce it as best he could. It would be a long time before he would get to sleep tonight.

★ ★ ★

It was barely daylight outside the Long S ranch. Stryker stood in front of his men. He had six of them there: Wingate, Lewis, Venters, 'Mack' McDonald, Joe Bloom and Big Sutter. They had all been dragged out of their beds before dawn so their collective mood was not the best. Surly would have been a way to describe their overall air. Not being stupid, Stryker knew this full well but, being the kind of man he was, he also knew how to rally their mood to his cause.

'Men, you're going on a mission to save your livelihoods. This Abbey Watt and Merrill Avery have been like a red rag to a bull for too long. Well, if you get in with the bull too long you're going to get gored.'

'You want us to rough them up?'

184

asked Big Sutter with a sort of gloomy relish, 'and do it real good?'

'Hear me out,' said Stryker patiently, knowing that he did not have long to get them on the road. If he showed any impatience it might well lead to refusals that he could do without. 'I've employed the six of you, along with many others over the years. With the spread of these homesteaders down the valley and over these lands, we're seeing the plains and trails get more and more enclosed. They're taking away our livelihood.'

'Bastards,' said Mack, a man with deep feeling for his job.

'These are the only jobs we've had for most of our lives. We're not shopkeepers, or carpetbaggers or saloonkeepers. We're range riders. And they're taking that away from us. So I want you to go down there, capture the pair of them and hang them from the white oak tree at the head of the valley. Simple as that. A graphic warning to them that wants to interfere with our way of life, else those meadows will never be ours and we'll never get to keep anything.'

'The law'll come after us,' said Venters, speaking for the first time.

'Not true,' said Stryker, 'I've seen to that personally. The law's elsewhere right now and I'm guessing they'll be mighty tied up for at least the next few hours.'

'But we'll be arrested anyway,' said Sutter, 'when the word gets out.'

'That's just it; you think the CTA don't have any teeth? We're the most powerful force in this county. You boys'll be protected. Now do this to save your jobs, boys, because only action will do that.'

The mood had settled now. The six men had been drawn by Stryker's sheer force of personality to do what he had asked. They knew full well that if they carried out the act it would scare a *lot* of people and they had been miserable and angry for a long time about the threat to their livelihood. Now they had a focus for their anger.

This was going to happen.

Stryker watched his men ride away, the hempen rope coiled in Lewis's saddle pack. He was more or less satisfied, and he wasn't lying to them. With those two dead, there would be a warning out there that would reverberate through the whole territory, not just Carbon County. Satisfied, he went inside to get his breakfast. He needed to fortify the inner man for the long day ahead.

For the law would be along at some point.

18

The sheriff and his deputy rode through the low scrubland and up the dusty trail that led to Jubal Thorne's new spread. Like Stryker and his men they were up just before dawn for a very different purpose. They were going to see a man who seemed to have brought nothing but death and lawbreaking to a once peaceful region. There had been the wars between the new settlers and the range riders, but these had been more like skirmishes. And from the look of it, Jubal Thorne was a hired hand brought in by Abbey Watt to secure her position in the valley and free her from interference by others who were protecting their own interests.

'Look here,' said Bud, 'ain't that a new grave?'

'Yep, it's where he must've stowed the old man,' said Matt. 'Sensible of him too given the weather's been warmer lately.'

'Well, it ain't warm now, Matt,' said Bud. This was true: before sunup the air was distinctly chilly. The dawn light was just drawing over the horizon and they could see their breath in front of their faces. The sheriff got his deputy to dismount before doing the same, and they led their horses towards the ramshackle ranch. Matt whispered a command to his companion and they left their horses where they were and went towards the building. They had both drawn their guns and were walking towards the porch, hoping that Thorne was still sleeping off his exertions from the days before. The rough, unpainted front door gave a creak as it swung slowly open.

'You two looking for me?' said a low but penetrating voice from behind them. They both turned, weapons at the ready.

Jubal Thorne was standing there, his long coat flapping a little in the morning breeze that hardly stirred his heavy, coppery hair, but that was not what caught their attention. It was the Peacemaker he held in either hand, the barrels levelled steadily at their bodies.

★ ★ ★

Cyrus was a determined young man. His father had been a drunk who made Cy work from an early age, earning enough money to keep his fond parent in liquor. When the pair had ended up working for Abbey Watt it had seemed like a solution from heaven. His father had somewhere secure to stay and Cy was well fed for the first time since his mother had succumbed to a fever six years before.

Then his father, old Joe, had been inconsiderate enough to drop dead from a heart attack while he was driving in some fence-poles with a sledgehammer. His system, weakened from years of boozing, had not been strong enough to withstand the extra pressure. This was ironic, because the only reason he had been working so hard was because he had set his cap at Abbey Watt. He had confided to his son once that 'she's a fine woman, and once we gets hitched I'll be on easy street.'

Well, that was never going to happen. But now that he was an orphan, Abbey Watt had become his mentor as well as his boss. In his own fierce and loyal way, he loved her and when she asked him to do a job he did that job well, even if it meant working with Merrill, who was a hard taskmaster.

The trouble with the irrigation ditches was that as the river went down after the winter rains subsided, there was a build-up of silt over the winter that absorbed much of the water that was supposed to run along to the ditches at the side of the fields. The only way to make sure the water flowed consistently was to clear the ditches out with a panned shovel that allowed him to scoop out large amounts of fine, wet soil.

Cy got up before dawn, rode to the

eatery and tethered his grey to a stretch of fence that led to the fields. He took down his short-handled shovel and got to work. There was no sign of Avery, but Cy just knew the big man would appear in a short while, shouting his useless orders and unwilling to get as dirty as his companion.

Billy was needed back at the ranch to see to the animals, mucking out the livery and putting in the fresh straw and leading the cattle down to the meadows.

Cy did not mind; he was quite happy to work on his own. The earth had a rich, loamy scent that filled his nostrils and there was a red line across the dawning sky. There was something about digging that made his youthful body feel good even though his muscles would be aching at the end of the day.

He felt alive.

In the channel he was largely concealed from view, and he was concentrating on his work, so the rumble of hoofs on the dirt road hardly struck him until the sound came closer. Instinctively he ducked down, knowing that now was not the time to draw attention to his own presence. The eatery was down the road from the ditch and the hoofs thundered past. There was the sound of rattling wheels as a buckboard passed too. He heard men talking to one another, and then the sound of hoofs halted.

Without even considering what he was doing, Cyrus climbed out of the irrigation channel, scrambled over the side, keeping low, and ran over to his horse.

He could hear men shouting and the protests of Merrill Avery, who was being bundled out of his own home and striking out with his fists as they took him.

Cyrus did not even look back. He knew if he tried to ride back past the men to warn Abbey he would be shot at and possibly killed. There was only one direction in which he could head. After riding for a minute he dared to look back and saw that Avery was being flung on the back of the cart. The men were silent now, grimly doing what they saw as their duty.

Urging his horse onwards by kicking with his heels and whispering encouragement, Cyrus headed out of the valley to the one man who would help them out of this predicament — and he knew that he had very little time left, if any.

★　★　★

'Well, Sheriff, I was just taking an early morning stroll when I heard noises. I figured it was time to see who was visiting me at this ungodly hour. Guess I don't need these.' The Peacemakers vanished from Thorne's hands as if he had done some kind of conjuring trick. He didn't wear a gun belt.

'Thorne, I'm going to make this easy on you,' said Matt Buck. 'Come back to town with us and you'll be in a nice warm jail cell in ten minutes. You'll even get a java for your troubles.'

'You see, Sheriff, I don't look at it

that way. You come barging onto my land and you say that you're going to arrest me without telling me what for.'

'Guess I owe you that much of a courtesy. You're a hired killer, Thorne; you came here a paid man to take down some of the big boys. You've been helping the new settlers — and some of the older ones from what I hear.'

'You've been hearing about the fences we took down,' said Thorne evenly. 'Well, I guess I knew there would be some trouble about that.'

'You've destroyed Wingate's claim.'

'Wingate doesn't have a claim, as you well know.'

'Along with Venters and Lewis, he seemed to think he did.'

'Tell you what, Sheriff, you had a visit last night from those three, didn't you?'

'Yup, sure did.'

'Tell me, was Mr Stryker with them?'

'What are you getting at, Thorne? And quit stalling,' said the sheriff.

'He was, wasn't he? So I guess it's the

justice of the big boys,' said Thorne. 'I paid a deposit for this land fair and square. I contacted Tom's son for him, made the arrangements for travel and I was the one who discovered that he had been murdered. I have legal documents too.'

'Then where's your lawyer?'

'You tell me, Sheriff. Looks like the lawyer vanished when someone with deep enough pockets was around to send him on his way.'

All the while he had been speaking, Thorne had been backing away from the ranch house towards a solidly built storage shed.

'He's trying to get away,' yelled Bud, raising his Colt. A shot rang out, but not from the deputy, and suddenly the gun in his hand leapt away from him like a living thing while the deputy wrung his hand in pain. He had not been shot but the force of the weapon being jerked away from him had hurt his hand badly.

At the same time as the shot arrived,

Thorne melted into the shadows as quickly as he had appeared. The sheriff ran forward to intercept the gunman while his deputy was still trying to recover from the pain of a sprained wrist.

'Thorne, you're just making it worse. Give up now.' The sun was beginning to rise, and in a moment the pool of darkness beside the outhouse would melt away, then the sheriff would be face to face with his newfound enemy. He was concentrating so much on the task before him that he barely heard the sound of horse hoofs pounding across the hard ground.

Then to his right, Cyrus the orphan came into view, his grey mare sweating from the hard journey.

'Jubal, you've got to come with me. They're going to be killed!'

19

Thorne stepped out of the shadows as the boy slid off his horse. Cyrus stood beside the sheriff, barely even seeming to notice that the man was there.

'Well,' said Thorne, coming closer to the lawman, 'this isn't good. I thought our Mr Stryker would hold off for a few days, but it looks as if he's a lot more enterprising than I thought. Sheriff, there's no time to lose. Come with me, we have to prevent a terrible crime from happening.'

'What? I see what this is: this kid was around here somewhere and you set it up with him to come to your rescue if needed.'

'Sheriff, that ain't what I'm doing here,' protested Cyrus.

'Shut up, kid,' said Matt, thrusting out his not inconsiderable jaw. He was the only one armed now because the

Peacemakers had melted away again.

'You're a blind idiot,' said Thorne. He was close enough to the sheriff that he could have touched the other man just by stretching out an arm. He stretched an arm out all right, stepping swiftly to one side and giving the sheriff a haymaker on the chin with a bony fist shielded by a leather glove. The sheriff gave a grunt of surprise and fired his gun into the shadows as his finger tightened on the trigger in an involuntary motion, and he fell to the ground. Thorne swiftly purloined the weapon, thrusting it into his pocket.

Bud, having recovered a little from the pain and seeing what had happened, dived for his weapon just as Cyrus ran forward, kicked the gun away from him and scrambled to pick it up. Bud, despite his sore wrist, dived on top of the boy and bore him to the ground and the two began to struggle for possession of the weapon. Thorne in no mood to waste time. He strode forward and pulled Bud away from the young man by the scruff of the neck using both hands. The young man seized the weapon. Thorne nodded approvingly.

'Cover him, Cyrus, and wait here.'

'I'm going with you.'

'No, you ain't,' said Thorne grimly. He did not waste any more time but drew up his own horse, cursing himself for not being more prepared. He had honestly been expecting the big land-owners to wait a few days before trying anything. He had underestimated his enemy. These were not the usual scum he had been used to bringing back in his days as a bounty hunter. These were men who were used to working hard and getting things done promptly. He had underestimated the enemy.

He flung the body of the still-unconscious sheriff across the saddle.

'Where are you taking him?' asked Bud.

'I'll need a really good witness,' replied Thorne.

'Hurry,' said Cyrus, almost weeping. 'Hurry, Jubal.'

The gunman brought his horse to where the two lawmen had tethered their own. He left the sheriff on Eb, just making sure that the officer was tethered there by the harness. He jumped on the sheriff's roan and, with a swift command to his own horse, rode down towards the valley as fast as he dared on the uneven ground. It would take one second for his horse to stumble and throw an unfamiliar rider, and then nobody would be rescued.

He only hoped they were going to be there in time to stop an atrocity.

* * *

'I've changed my mind,' said Wingate just after Cyrus had departed. He and his men had been so busy concentrating on what they were doing that they had not noticed the departure of the boy, the irrigation channels being at the head of the road that led to the eatery. Now Avery was on the buckboard, kicking out his heels and yelling in protest. 'Bring him here. Look at those trees just in front of the food house. Reckon it's going to make a few people think if they see this dog and that bitch hanging there right in front of them. Go get her and we'll carry out the task as soon as.'

He had Avery gagged so that they would hear nothing more from the aggrieved landowner, and departed to fetch Abbey Watt.

She was up at dawn as usual, tending to the animals and carrying out one or other of the endless tasks that came with having your own spread and very little in the way of help, when the men arrived. She took one look at the riders, all of who had concealed their faces with bandanas, and knew instantly what they were there for. Dropping the basket of eggs that she had just collected from the many chickens that scratched around the farmyard, she ran for the building where her weapons were stored. But it was too late; two of the men dropped off and grabbed her by the arms.

Billy, who was in the barn, ran out holding a pitchfork he had been using to gather hay for the horses. He had no sense of strategy but headed straight for the men who were holding his employer, trying to spear one of them with the fork. He was halted by a blow to the back of the head with the butt of a gun from Wingate, the hit bringing him to his knees. He dropped the fork and collapsed on to his face.

'Don't shoot him,' Abbey screamed. She was a big, strong woman. She struck out at them, managing to throw one of the men to the ground. It just happened to be Venters, who gave a cry of rage, got to his feet and struck her a blow on the temple with the butt of his gun that sent her reeling. The other men seized her by the arms and began to drag her forward.

'Should we do something here?' asked Mack, looking at the woman's skirts. 'Give her somethin' to remember just before she hangs?'

'No,' Wingate grated out the word.

'This diseased bitch is going to go straight to hell and she ain't going to infect any of us.' The three men dragged the semi-conscious woman across to the buckboard where they threw her aboard. Mack went in beside her and held the flopping woman face down by sitting astride her and pushing her face into the grainy wood. She tried to cry out but her voice was muffled due to way her face was being pressed against the wagon.

'You crossed the big man one too many times,' said Wingate. He was seated at the front, holding the reins. He twisted his neck to look at the still-protesting woman. 'You were right though, whore, I never had a claim, not really.' He cracked his short whip and the horses trotted forward, heading back towards the eatery.

Soon she would be nothing but a graphic warning of what happened if you crossed Stryker and his associates at the Cattle Trading Association.

★ ★ ★

Thorne arrived on more even ground, with Eb still behind him carrying the semi-conscious sheriff. Just before they got to the valley, Thorne lifted his water canteen and poured some of the precious liquid on the sheriff's head.

'Wakey wakey,' he said grimly. The sheriff gave a shudder and slid off the saddle.

'Get back on your own horse like a man and follow me,' said Thorne. He was not wasting any time, and he knew the sheriff would follow, not because he was obeying the gunman, but because he was trailing a dangerous man.

Thorne did not even look back at what the sheriff was doing as his own powerful animal coursed forward down the trail that led to the Avery spread. Quite a few minutes had passed since his encounter with Cyrus, and his greatest fear was that he would arrive far too late.

There, in the fresh light of dawn as the sun was just rising above the hills, he saw one of the worst sights he had ever encountered in his life. Abbey and her partner were seated on stamping horses beneath a chestnut tree that had sturdy, outspread branches. Looped around those branches, secured with a hitch knot, were two white hempen ropes of the finer type often used on the big ranches for roping animals. They were being put to a far more sinister purpose now. Wingate was facing the two captives, still masking his features with a bandanna — as were all the other men. It was obvious that he was about to give the order that would make two of his companions whip the horses that held both captive, making them start forward and hang the couple.

Neither of the two had been hooded — that was a final mercy only given by a real hangman — but both had been gagged so that they could not protest at what was happening. It was also a way of stopping them from influencing anyone who might have thought twice about what they were doing.

Thorne turned and flung the sheriff

the weapon he had taken from him just a short while ago.

'Back me up,' he said, throwing back his coppery hair, his hat flying off as he did so. This exposed that terrifying, skeletal part of his features that had so disconcerted the men before. Instead of a gun he pulled out his Bowie knife from the side of his boot and urged his steed forward while giving a wordless shout at the top of his lungs.

The men who had been standing to urge the horses forward, turned and saw a grinning, demonic figure in black coming towards them, panicked and began to run over the grass, forgetting about the guns at their sides. Wingate saw too and gave a loud shout of anger. He pulled out his Colt .45 and discharged it, not at the new arrival, but into the air just above the heads of the horses that bore the luckless couple. As he expected the horses started forward — and the couple were hung!

They spun on the end of their ropes, dying in front of the new arrival.

Thorne knew something that no one else there would even have considered. These were trail riders, not professional executioners and the ropes they were using had not been calibrated in the way a hangman would have had them.

The sheriff shot at the group of men. Besides being panicked by the new arrival, they realized that they had been caught and fled en masse, including Wingate: as far as he was concerned, he did not need to stay and fight now that his job was done. Wingate groaned in pain — he had been wounded on his left side. However, he also took one last shot at the sheriff and was lucky enough to startle Matt's horse so that the luckless lawman was thrown heavily to the ground.

The lynch mob ran forward, men scrambling back on to their mounts and riding away from the valley as fast as they had arrived.

In the meantime, still mounted on Eb, Thorne went straight up to Avery and slashed out with his ultra-sharp knife, parting the rope as if it was twine. Avery was a big man, and the fall to the ground a few feet below might hurt him, but it was better than choking to death, which was exactly what he was doing. The knife slashed through the taut rope in a second or two. He did not even wait to see the big man fall, but turned to the woman and slashed the rope that was throttling the life out of her, this time managing to support her with his wiry arms as he promptly dropped the knife and grabbed hold of her limp body.

He slid off the saddle, laid her to the ground and then ran between the trees, pulling the Peacemakers out as he did so, but he need not have bothered. The enemy had already vanished, satisfied that they had carried out their orders, with only a thick cloud of dust in the distance obscuring them from view.

From the stillness of the two bodies on the ground, it looked as if they had succeeded in their mission.

20

Stryker was practically foaming at the mouth as his men stood, one or two with their heads bowed.

'What do you mean, 'Thorne arrived'?'

'It was like nothing on earth,' said Venters, most superstitious of them all. 'Like the devil incarnate on that big black horse of his.'

'But you say you managed to hang 'em? That's the important bit.'

'We sure did,' said Mack enthusiastically. 'Them two, Abbey Watt and her man, they're goners for sure.'

'And you're sure the sheriff didn't see any of your faces?' asked Stryker.

'No,' said Lewis, 'I was real careful that we always kept covered up.'

'Then when the sheriff returns and comes here to investigate, as far as I'm concerned you've all been working,' said Stryker. 'You can all go back to work now, and you'll get your bonus. As far as I'm concerned, we've sent out the right message. Those settlers won't even want to come near Clearwater now that they know what they're up against.'

Once they were gone he did not go back to his own comfortable home, where he lived with his compliant, younger wife and two young daughters. Instead he went to the bunkhouse, where Wingate lay, having been tended to by one of Stryker's housemaids with his wounded side bandaged up. Wingate lay on his bunk with a scornful look on his narrow features. He gave a groan as he tried to sit up when Stryker entered.

'Just lie around like a lazy hound,' said Stryker jovially.

'Well, a man likes a bit of leisure now and then,' said Wingate, though he was gritting his teeth against the pain.

'Honestly, Dabs, when you arrived I thought you were a goner with all that blood,' said Stryker. 'Did the girl see to you?'

'Yep, cleaned me up and sewed the

wound together; it's only a scratch. Luckily that Matt Buck can't aim for taffy,' said the wounded cowboy.

'If that stupid sheriff comes around asking awkward questions, you won't be here.'

'What do you mean?'

'You'll be on furlough, visiting your sister upstate,' said Stryker.

'I get it.'

'You did well,' said Stryker, 'despite having that pain in the ass arrive and nearly mess up things for us all.'

'That's the thing,' said Wingate, 'we might still have ballsed it up regarding what happened.'

'What do you mean?'

'The others, they was too busy being scared and scrambling away to save their own skins, but I was facing him. He didn't have a gun in his hand, nothing but a big old knife.'

'A knife?'

'And when they was hanging he moved between them.'

'Did you see what happened?'

'That's the thing; it gets all kind of hazy. I was riding forward, trying to aim back at that mad sheriff, who had just shot me. I shot back and Buck went off his horse then the pain got me. It was good old Trail boy, my horse, who got me out of there. He just cantered off while I was passing out in the saddle, and you know he's real fast.'

Stryker digested the news in silence. He was not a stupid man; he knew that if Thorne had arrived with a sharp enough knife that had been used to slash the ropes, there was a chance — however small — that the lives of the two ranchers might have been saved.

'Then we have no choice: we'll have to sit tight for a couple of days to hear what news comes in, then we'll have to go back and finish the job we started.'

'Can't we just leave things as they are?'

'No!' Stryker punched his right fist into his left hand. 'I'm the head of the association. If word gets out we've been bested by a hired killer and a couple of settlers it will be the end. We've got to show our hand.'

'I guess I'll be up and about in a couple of days,' said Wingate. 'I'm in. You see, if it hadn't been for Thorne I wouldn't be hurt like this. It was him brought the sheriff to us when he shoulda been in gaol.'

'Thanks, and this time none of them'll get away,' said Stryker. 'Six men and one leader is all it takes. See you, Dabs.' He turned on his heel and left the bunkhouse, a set expression on his face that did not bode well for Thorne and his companions. If Wingate was correct, this had to be dealt with right away. He could only hope that the job had been done right. Even without the bodies being left hanging in the breeze for all to see, the deaths of Abbey Watt and Merrill Avery would be a potent symbol of what anyone who crossed him could expect.

They would act as a warning.

★ ★ ★

Thorne did what he could, paying attention to the still woman first, lifting her to her feet, the ache in his back almost stopping him from doing so. She was limp, seeming almost lifeless.

'Abbey,' he said forcefully, 'you can't let them win.' He began to walk and she gave a groan, then her eyes fluttered open like those of someone who had been in a deep sleep. She gave a groan and began to move with him, her breathing coming in shallow gasps. For what seemed like forever, but must have been a couple of minutes, he walked her beside the trees. Then, satisfied that she was recovering, he allowed her to sit at the grassy base of a beech and turned his attentions to Merrill.

Thorne examined the big man. Merrill's colour was not good, but then his features had always been on the red side. Thorne pressed on the big man's fleshy chest a few times, and was rewarded with a gasp from what had seemed like a dead body. Avery opened his eyes and stared upwards, barely believing that he was still there.

'Hell, that hurts,' said the sheriff, groaning as he lay on the ground, his horse remaining nearby as he nursed his injured leg. Thorne came over and had a quick look at the damage.

'I think it's broken,' he said. 'We'll just have to get you into Avery's home.'

There was the sound of thundering hoofs, and the gunman immediately leapt away from the injured man, pulling out his weapons as he did so and sheltering behind the very tree from which the lynch mob had tried to hang the luckless pair. He had one advantage in that a man on the ground would be able to pick off any arrivals more easily than they would be able to shoot him. It was never easy to aim accurately when on horseback.

Only two people arrived, Cyrus and Bud, with the deputy in the lead. They both jumped off their respective mounts and Cyrus ran towards the couple, while Bud soon found the side of the sheriff. The deputy had his gun out and glared wildly around for would-be foes.

'What the hell have they done, Matt?'

'It's all right,' said the sheriff, before emitting another loud groan, 'they're on our side. Don't shoot Thorne.'

The gunman stepped from between the trees. He still had his Peacemakers in his hands. By this time he had restored his hair and eye patch, but there was a wild look about him that might have put the new arrival against him. The deputy was so keyed up that Thorne was worried he might still react badly.

'It's what he says; I have nothing to do with this. Put the gun away. We have far more urgent things to do than fight amongst ourselves.'

Looking at the injured sheriff and the couple who had been rescued, Bud saw the sense of this and holstered his gun. Along with Cyrus, he proved that he might not be the brightest of men, but he was young and strong, well able to follow orders.

'Cy was convinced there was somethin' going on,' said Atkins. 'I decided to let him come back here.'

They made a makeshift stretcher out of some canvas and wood and assisted the sheriff into the building on it. In the meantime Cyrus helped Abbey Watt into the building, then he and Thorne assisted Avery into his own home, having to prop up the big man for fear that he would fall and injure himself, so unsteady was he on his feet.

Abbey proved herself to be made of stronger stuff than Thorne would have thought. This was a woman who had barely survived a hanging, but as they brought the glassy-eyed Avery in and sat him down it was clear that she was already recovering from her ordeal as well as anyone in that situation could. Her voice was hoarse when she spoke, but she had already drunk some water and she was looking at Thorne with her hands on her hips.

'This ain't finished, is it?'

'No, ma'am,' said Thorne thoughtfully, 'I guess it's just beginning.'

21

Billy groaned and turned over about half an hour after the events that had laid him out. The men had long taken Abbey Watt.

His first thought was so much for the weapons that had been brought to them the previous day. Billy had wanted to use those guns, being too young to realize the import of what he would be doing if he shot at experienced range riders. Now he was unable to take his chance.

He was filled with rage at what they had done to his female boss. Abbey Watt had shown him nothing but kindness during his time with her and he hadn't seen a lot of that in his young life. His father had been a veteran of the Civil War who had made his young wife pregnant and then vanished, never to be seen again. Billy's mother had been forced to do a lot of menial work just to survive, leaving the child with a senile grandmother who barely took care of him. He had grown up with hardly any education and a lot of brawn. Then his mother, old beyond her years, had died of a winter fever just after his grandmother succumbed to the same fate, and he had ended up in an orphanage just outside town. There he had been treated as slave labour, so at thirteen when he had been sent to help Abbey build her new ranch on loan, he had been given a new chance.

At first, with all the hard work that he had to do along with Cyrus and the latter's father it had seemed like more of the same, but when Abbey had petitioned for him to become her full-time worker the idea gradually penetrated that he was onto a good thing.

Thanks to Merrill's eatery, where he helped out, he was fed regularly and began to fill out and shoot upwards, so that by the age of fifteen he was a big, strapping lad — as he had proven when he helped to remove the fencing just the day before.

Now he ran into the farmhouse and loaded the two Winchesters, the handguns and the ammunition into a canvas bag, which he threw across his back. With trembling hands he loaded bullets into one of the handguns — a Colt .44 service revolver — that, like all of the weapons Avery had been able to muster, had seen better days. Then he jumped on a gelding that was in a skittish mood, having not been fed that morning due to the circumstances, and kicked with his heels and rode hard towards the other building.

The trouble was his horse was not in the mood to be treated this way, and went only so far before bucking wildly at being mistreated. If Billy had taken things easier it would have been better for them both.

Billy was flung from the back of his horse and hit the ground with some force, his head striking against the fencing in that area. He was knocked out and the bag of weaponry lay yards away from him where it had landed, meaning neither the young man or the armaments could do any good for those he had wanted to rescue.

He awoke a while later to find that he was still in the same place where he had fallen. He knew that a great deal of time had passed because the noise of the men carrying out the hanging of the luckless couple had long since ceased, and the sun was higher in the sky. His horse was cropping some juicy grass nearby. Cursing, he got slowly to his feet, groaning as he did so, picked up the weapons and headed towards the eatery, this time leading the animal by the reins and limping painfully along.

★ ★ ★

Starry walked casually out of the saloon and went to the Brewlins Hotel. He had some bad news for a good friend of his. He was a big, good-looking man in his early thirties, and when she saw him come into the building she met him with a bright smile of welcome, which he did not return.

'You got time to talk, Lena?' he asked.

'For you, Jack, any time's a good time.'

'This is real bad news,' he said as they went outside and he led her to the side of the building. 'I thought I'd better tell you first.'

'What is it?' She was struck by how serious he was: usually when she was in his company his mood was light and humorous. In fact he was the kind of man she would very much like to settle down with in the future, and from the way things were going it had looked as if he would ask the right question in due course. But all humour was gone now as he looked down at her pretty face.

'Looks as if that spot of trouble we were talking about ain't going to blow over at all.'

'You're talking about Abbey, aren't

you?' This time there was real alarm in her voice.

'You could say that. Thing is no one thought it would happen at all, that there would be threats but no action.'

'I need to know.' Her eyes searched his face for an answer.

'Guess it's just the way things go down when the big boys decide that they're going to take down the small guy,' said Starry, 'but it's brutal, real brutal. This morning a bunch of riders went down the valley, captured Merrill and Abbey and hung them from a tree outside the eatery.' There was a moment of stunned silence from the young woman, and then her face began to crumple as the full import of the words hit her.

'The bastards, the evil bastards. She was my friend.' The tears flooded from her eyes, but she wiped them aside almost scornfully. 'How do you know?'

'Old Dud Watkins was up early, working his fields over from Merrill's property. When he saw the gang arrive he hid in his own field, saw the couple getting ready to be hanged and crawled away until he was on the other side of the hill, then ran to his own farmhouse. He came into town there all shaken, had to get a drink, and told me how he saw the ropes around their necks and everything as they was putting them on the horses. He's in there now.'

'Why didn't he do something?' she demanded with eyes that now glared at Starry, tears forgotten in a flood of anger.

'Whoa, I'm not to blame,' he said, stepping back, 'and neither is he. When six armed men are hanging your neighbours, if they think there's a witness, then you might be next.'

She could not blame Watkins, an older man who sometimes came into the hotel for a drink of a night. He was a harmless man with a younger wife and a little son, both of whom were away visiting relatives. He would not want to take the chance of depriving that son of a father, nor his wife of a husband.

'He's in there now, trying to drink this away.'

'It was those cattle traders, wasn't it? They've accused her of all sorts, of being a whore in this very hotel, of being a cattle rustler, a common thief, but I've known her for years: a more peaceable, hard-working, honest person I've never known.'

'There's nothing we can do,' said Starry, 'but watch out. Stryker is a clever man; he'll put his own mark on this. He'll say how sorry he is that this happened, and it's a terrible thing that's bringing the territory into disrepute, but he'll have his claim on that land in less than a month.' He looked at her thoughtfully. 'There's only one thing: he reported something strange.'

'What was that?'

'Dud looked back as he was riding away, just after he heard the horsemen riding off, and he was passing the eatery but at a distance. The bodies were lying on the ground, and there was a wild-looking man in black with dark red hair standing near them.'

'Bodies on the ground? I thought they were hung rather than shot. Then Watkins left and he's been in here drinking ever since . . . '

'That's the point — the ropes had been cut by someone's hand.'

'Thorne,' said Lena. She looked directly at Starry. 'Then there's hope.'

'But even if they did survive I guess there's not much we can do.'

'There's a whole lot of townspeople would disagree with you, Jack,' she said, using his first name. 'It's time we kept our eyes open and helped those who need our aid.'

'But it's big business; they'll ruin us,' said Starry.

'Maybe, but there are ways. Have you ever heard the phrase 'fighting fire with fire?' '

'Maybe.'

She gave him her sweetest smile and suddenly he felt her arms around him, and for a moment their problems melted away.

22

Matt Buck had tried to be stoic, but he still screamed one or twice as his broken leg was bound, the pain barely muted by the half bottle of bourbon whiskey he had consumed during the process. Abbey Watt had done what she could with the materials at hand using cloth strips and a length of hard wood on either side of the fracture to keep the bone together.

'You did a good job,' said Thorne. They were in the master bedroom of Avery's home, which was far more ornate than that of her own ranch building, with prints on the walls and even polished wooden flooring. Merrill Avery had obviously done well out of his business.

'You rest, Sheriff,' she said. The man, obviously still suffering as he lay on the bed, turned his face to the wall and said nothing.

Thorne walked with her out of the room and they went through the big, open front living area where Merrill still sat in his oversized rocking chair, his face ashen as he recovered from the ordeal that had nearly killed him. Nearby, in a leather armchair cradling his gun, was Bud Atkins, chewing anxiously at his lower lip.

'I ought to go to his spread and arrest Stryker right now,' said Bud. 'Trouble is, there's no proof that it was his men. He'd laugh right in my face.'

'Where's Cy?' asked Abbey. 'He's not off to do something stupid, is he?'

'They've had the upper hand and now they know it,' said Bud, ignoring her and staring into space. He had seen a lot of action for a young man but had never been faced with this kind of raw power before. The big boys were showing their hand now that they had been crossed and it scared him more than he was prepared to admit.

'I have to leave,' Abbey told Thorne. 'I have to find out what's happened to

Billy. I don't know what they've done to him.'

'I guess Cy was thinking the same thing,' said Thorne. 'You mentioned Billy earlier and he's off to see if he can find his buddy.' They soon had their answer, because Cy appeared in the yard with Billy limping beside him. Cy had taken over the burden of carrying the weapons and there was a grim expression on his face.

Abbey was about to go out and join them, but Thorne pulled her back.

'Let me do this.' She knew straight away that he was protecting her in case there was going to be another attack.

'There's no one there except for the boys.'

'I'll be the judge of that,' he said. 'I've dealt with treachery before.' The way he said the words sent a sudden chill through her body. This was a man who knew the truth of how things happened out here. Injustice was a way of life for many, and the so-called law had nearly been responsible for her death by trying to arrest the one man who had been able to save her.

Thorne went out, armed with his guns, slipping from the shadows and watching out for whoever might be there. Satisfied, he pocketed his weapons, helped the new arrivals stable their horses and carried the weapons back inside.

'You two, what have you been up to?' Abbey began scolding the two young men, then stood aside and let them enter. 'Get inside, I don't want to see you out of my sight again until this blows over.' She saw the way the young man was limping. 'What happened to you, Billy?'

'I was in a hurry and got thrown off my horse,' he said. 'Nearly broke my neck.'

'Well, I'll break your neck if you do anything stupid,' she said. But the tone in her voice and the look in her eyes showed that she was glad to have all her men back together again.

'It's no use,' said a deep, slow voice from the direction of the rocking chair. 'We got to get out, and they've won.'

Avery had spoken.

'What do you think, Jubal Thorne?' asked Abbey.

'What do I think?' He stood and surveyed the two anxious young men who stood there, the deputy who seemed sunk in his own thoughts, the dull-eyed man who rocked in his chair and stared forward with distant eyes that had seen death, and thought of the man who was groaning in the master bedroom. 'I think Avery's right,' said Thorne. 'You should all get out of here, just leave it all behind and fight them through the courts.'

'Or else?'

'Let's just say you can stay and fight, but there'll be a bloody battle and I can't guarantee what will happen, except for one thing.'

'And what is that?'

'There's going to be a lot of trouble if we stay put.'

★   ★   ★

It was just before dawn the following day in a pass that led from Stryker's property down to Clearwater Valley. There was a gathering of men and horses, shadowy figures in the grey light that filtered from across the hills of Carbon County.

Stryker looked at his men, all of whom were ready, bandanas round their necks to act as masks. They were all there, Lewis, Venters, Sutter, Big Mack, and Joe Bloom, all of whom had taken part in the previous attack on Avery and his companion. Only Wingate was missing, not having been summoned to the task due to his injuries.

'I could have got a dozen more men to do this job,' said Stryker. 'All I needed was to ask some of the other members of the Cattle Trader's Association and we'd have been all set.'

'Why didn't you then, boss?' asked Lewis, a man who lacked a great deal of insight. Stryker spread out his hands.

'Don't you see this has gone far enough as it is? I can't rely on those blabbermouths to get involved in this, and there'll be an investigation into this once the law in other counties and the administration of the territory take an interest.'

'What kind of investigation?'

'The law *will* be involved; boy, they will be. If we keep this nice and simple, get it all done as it should be, all we need to do once it's all over is sit nice and tight.'

'That's all right for you to say,' Joe Bloom suddenly spoke up. He had not been personally involved before and had never met Thorne. 'We're the ones risking our necks while you get to sit in your little kingdom up here.'

'That's where you're wrong,' said Stryker. 'This situation's too urgent to be left to a few riders more used to herding cattle.'

'Hey!' said Lewis, stung to the core by this.

'Jim, you know what I mean,' said Stryker. 'What you men need is a little bit of leadership, and that's what I'm here for now that Wingate is missing.' He looked at them from under lowered brows. 'Not that it's for the money, I would hope that you guys would be loyal enough to settle this as a way of keeping your way of life, but I'm going to treble the bonus I've offered you already.'

Three month's wages! There was a stirring amongst the men at this; most of them couldn't see past the money. Some of them had families, or girls they wanted to marry. This would be a way of doing what they wanted.

There was a steady clopping of hoofs, and a rider came around the bend in the grey light of morning sitting stiffly on his roan. Instantly some handguns were drawn on him, but sitting there rigidly he uttered a cry to identify who he was.

'Don't shoot; I wouldn't miss this for anything. He's getting taken down.'

'You want to kill the sheriff?' asked Stryker.

'No, that bastard Thorne; he's the

cause of this, really. He's finished.'

'As long as you think you can keep up with us,' said Stryker.

For some reason the new arrival had made the mission real for the remainder of the men. They put their bandanas across their faces and made their way in a string out to the main trail with Wingate, their real leader, at the front.

23

Avery was still in his rocking chair. He had barely stirred in the last few hours, had even slept there all night. The big living space was empty except for one other occupant, Abbey Watt, who looked at her aging partner in the flickering light of the oil lamp on the table between them.

'I guess this is it,' she said. 'I just want to say that I'm sorry for all the trouble I've brought on you.'

'Where is everybody?' asked Avery slowly, as if speaking in a dream.

'I sent all your workers home yesterday. Told them you were ill,' said Abbey briskly. 'Not so far from the truth. The boys are upstairs, one at each far window. Bud is in the barn, and as for Thorne . . . ' her voice became flat, 'he's outside too.'

'You don't need to take on so,' said

Avery, 'about the land I mean. You wanted to get out there. You had ambition and you worked. Oh, how you worked.' The big man fell silent as if looking into his own mind and not liking much what he saw there. 'I'm the one who brought this on us all; I should've been content with what I had.'

'No you shouldn't,' she said fiercely, 'I got into this with both eyes open. I'm the one who made them come down on us like this. We only just survived due to an intervention from that man out there. They won't take us again.' She went over to the table in front of the window and picked up the Winchester that lay there. 'I've never fired a weapon in anger in my entire life. But I've hunted to survive, and I can shoot as well as any man.'

Behind her, Merrill Avery bowed his head in despair while the woman he had loved for so long cradled the weapon in her arms, looked out of the window and waited for what was to come.

* * *

The masked men rode into the valley and passed the eatery, the doors of which were shut, a notice proclaiming 'CLOSED due to illness.' They did not ride hastily or fast. The biggest man of all got off his horse and walked boldly towards the front of the ranch house.

'Abbey Watt,' he said, standing there with his legs apart, puffing out his chest, 'we'll give you one more chance. Get out of here with Avery and leave town. You'll get a fair price for the land.'

There was a moment when a curtain parted and a faint voice spoke.

'Get to hell. I know who you are, Stryker.' It was Abbey, who did not expose herself to fire.

'See, if you had left yesterday this would all be over; now it's still going to finish, but in a different way. You should have fled when you had the chance.' The big man moved away, retreating from the building and out of shot, nodding to his men as he did so. They all dismounted from their steeds, except for Wingate, who sat there rigidly, the pain just below the surface of his narrow features.

'Fan out and attack the building,' said Stryker to his remaining men. 'Dabs will keep a look-see with me right now. Just do what you have to do.' The men all nodded, fired up with the thought that they were protecting their jobs and their futures, and influenced by the malign power of the man himself. It was strange, but a powerful leader could make decent human beings behave in a way they would normally not have dreamed of doing. There was a code in the West that no man should lay a finger on a woman, and none of them would have dreamed of showing violence towards their wives or girlfriends, but Abbey Watt was not a woman to them: she was a creature who stood between them and their liveli-hoods, who needed to be stamped down on and exterminated, the way you would exterminate a bobcat who was preying on young cattle.

'I wouldn't do this if I was you,' said a powerful voice from above them. The men looked around with sudden fear. Venters made the sign of the cross. Stryker was the first to look in the direction from which the voice came. There, on the flat roof of the eatery, stood Jubal Thorne.

Hatless, with his coppery hair swept aside to show his features, eye patch gone too, he stood and glared at them, his long black coat flapping in the morning breeze, a Peacemaker in each hand.

'Now get on your horses and get out of here,' he said. 'You'll atone for the rest of your crimes another time.'

'The hell with you,' screamed Stryker, goaded beyond belief by the sight of the newcomer. 'You've ruined everything for me. Get him.' But his men seemed paralyzed with fear. All except for Wingate who suddenly cracked the reins of his blue and rode hard towards the eatery.

'Cover me,' he yelled at Stryker. The latter raised his gun and aimed straight at Thorne, firing a shot that would have nailed the gunman through the heart. But Thorne was no longer there. He seemed to have vanished like the villain in a pantomime, and for much the same reason. One moment he was in front of them, and then the shot was whistling through empty air to the spot where he had been. Venters made the sign of the cross again.

'We'll handle this,' snarled Stryker. 'Get on with it, see to the bitch.' He pounded over the grass between the trees.

Stryker was no stranger to the eatery. He knew that there were hatches that led straight to the roof of the building and that Thorne must have been standing beside one of these. He was running forward even as the main door of the eatery swung open and Thorne appeared, gun in either hand. Wingate appeared and tried to ride the man down, but Thorne dodged behind a tree and fired a shot just above the horse's head.

Wingate was flung off his mount and

fell to the ground where he lay, perhaps badly injured. It was hard for Stryker to tell. Stryker was a good shot. He took shelter behind one of the trees and took a hasty shot at his enemy. The bullet hit the tree beside which Thorne stood, thudding into the bark and sending splinters flying everywhere. Thorne reacted by taking shelter behind the very same tree on the far side from Stryker. They were now at an impasse, because if Stryker emerged he would be shot and if Thorne tried to move the result would be the same.

'You can walk away from this,' yelled Stryker. 'Get going in the same direction and you'll be out of here in no time. This ain't your fight.'

'I don't trust you,' yelled back Thorne. 'Besides, you made it my fight the day you killed Old Tom.'

'Then you're a dead man too,' said Stryker, a man who liked to keep his promises.

* * *

In the meantime the rest of the men attacked the main building, except for Lewis, who seemed to have vanished. It would not be long before their booted feet would kick in the front door. But as they advanced, a figure emerged from the barn. It was Bud Atkins; the young man held a gun in either hand, having borrowed the second from the sheriff.

'Surrender. You're finished. I speak with the authority of the law in these parts.' Venters turned and with a snarl stepped in front of the deputy.

'Supposing we just call it quits.'

'Can't do that. Now, put down your weapons.'

'No,' said a pleasant voice from behind him, 'you should've counted better, Atkins. Now drop them weapons.' Impelled by the feel of cold steel in the middle of his back, Atkins did as he was asked, his weapons thudding to the dry ground. A blow above his left ear completed the task and he fell to the ground, with Lewis stepping outside after doing the deed.

There was the sound of a window-pane being broken and this time the voice of Abbey Watt was clear.

'Not one step further or one of you dies.'

The riders fanned out then, with Venters running to one side of the main door. He was almost halted in his tracks by a shot that came from above. The boys were on either side of the house, looking down. They were both armed. It looked as if this was one mission that would not be accomplished after all. But the truth was, and Venters knew this, that if they were to succeed they had to do it now. The whole town would know who had done the deed.

Once the law from out of the county became involved there would be a crackdown on the trading association that would mean this could never happen again.

'Get them, boys,' he said to the men who had sheltered in the barn or behind one of the outbuildings. The men, including Lewis, began to fire at the two young men, who had sought to protect the main building. The boys had to withdraw or they would have been killed instantly. Venters knew it was hard for the woman inside to keep track of him from her side of the building and he ran in a manner that allowed him to approach the front door at an angle. She loosed a couple of shots and they came perilously close, but she missed him twice and by then he was so close to the building that she was unable to hit him. With a roar of triumph Venters kicked the door and burst into the building, gun in hand, just as the woman was turning from the window. He dimly glimpsed an ashen-faced man in a rocking chair and heard a groan from elsewhere as he burst into the building, but he had her clear in his sights now. Abbey Watt, their enemy, was about to die.

24

'You think this is the way?' called out Thorne. 'Your day is coming to an end, Stryker. Give up now or you're going to be as dead as the pillars that hold up that porch.'

'*You're* the dead man,' said Stryker. Infuriated by Thorne's words he swiftly exposed his body and took a shot at the tree behind which Thorne was sheltering. There was a click as he tried to fire another shot straight after the first. His gun had jammed. It had not been used for a while and the force of the bullets he had already fired had caused the barrel to heat and contract fast. A jam was not what he needed, but Thorne did not waste any time. Taking full advantage of the situation, the gunman cleared the space between them in a few seconds.

'Got you now, Stryker,' he said,

jamming his weapon against the ranch-er's chest. Thorne had been waiting patiently for the rancher to run out of bullets, goading him to fire off the last of his ammunition; the jamming of the weapon had merely had the same effect.

'Drop it,' said Thorne. He was dimly aware of the sound of horses' hoofs in the distance and a thought crossed his mind that perhaps some reinforcements were arriving for Stryker, but he had to control this situation right now. Stryker dropped the weapon.

'Now, we're going to march over there and we're going to put an end to this,' said Thorne grimly. 'Turn around and walk.' But even as he said the words, he saw an almost imperceptible widening of Stryker's eyes, these being the only part of his face visible due to the bandana that covered most of his features. Thorne felt that tingling between his shoulder blades that had saved his life so many times. He turned swiftly and found that he was facing Wingate, who was mere feet away.

'This woulda been settled,' snarled the distinctly battered-looking rider, 'if you hadn't been here.' Wingate wasted no more time, but shot at his enemy. Only Thorne, even as the words were said, lifted his right hand and fired a retaliatory shot that caught Wingate in the middle of the body. The rider was flung backwards, a red flower blossoming in the middle of his chest. He collided with his back against the very tree behind which Thorne had been hiding. He sagged downwards and this time he would not be rising again.

The shot that had been aimed at Thorne, who had twisted away like a cat, had hit the very man whom Wingate was trying to protect. Stryker was lying on the ground, his bandana had slipped off his face and he was grimacing in pain. Thorne had no time to wait; he examined the big man and saw that Stryker had been wounded on the shoulder. It must have been like being smacked with a hammer at that range.

Thorne made the big man get to his feet.

'For God's sake, I need a doctor,' said Stryker.

'You'll get one,' said Thorne, 'but first you're going to end all this.' He jammed his Peacemakers against the big man's back, and Stryker stumbled forward to the main building where the riders were still laying siege. Thorne stood behind the big man and his voice rang out loud and clear. 'OK boys, time to end this or your man here is a goner. Tell them, Stryker.'

'The hell with it.' The big rancher's voice buzzed with pain. 'I never figured on dying in bed anyway. Don't mind me, men. Kill this bastard. I don't care how I go. Just get him!'

* ★ *

Abbey Watt was turning slowly and it would only take a heartbeat to destroy her. Venters lifted his handgun. The Winchester was more ponderous and

250

the time it would take to lift and aim the weapon was just enough for him to blow her head off her shoulders. He saw the look of fear in her eyes. 'My boys,' she said, thinking of the two orphans even in this extreme. There was a loud bang as a weapon was discharged, and Venters looked down to see there was a hole that had punched straight through his body. The weapon clattered to the polished floor and Venters pitched forward onto his face, a pool of blood spreading around his recumbent body. Sheriff Matt Buck stood in the doorway, face twisted in pain, the smoking gun in his hand.

'It's not over,' he said.

★ ★ ★

Thorne heard the shot from inside the building and his mouth set in a grim line. He had never come across some-one who would order his own death just to serve an ideal, but then he himself had fought for his own ideals many times.

He stepped back, holding his Peacemakers wide and prepared for what would probably be his death. But the clattering of hoofs was closer now. Another four masked riders appeared: reinforcements after all, by the look of things. They were all masked as the previous riders had been. But one of them had a distinctly soft, rounded appearance, and all four riders dismounted swiftly and stood beside Thorne. They were all armed.

He was no longer a lone gunman.

'What are you waiting for?' yelled Stryker. 'Shoot them, kill them all!'

But that was the moment the tide turned against the unmasked man. Sheriff Matt Buck appeared in the doorway of the building. His leg was strapped and it was obvious that he was in great pain as he made his way across the yard.

'Kill him!' screamed Stryker, losing all control. The big man started to move, to hit out on his own, but he was grabbed by a forceful hand by the scruff of the neck and felt the cold steel of a

Peacemaker in his back again.

'It's finished,' said Thorne.

As he spoke the remaining riders came out and flung down their weapons. They, too surrendered, knowing that any fight they put up in the light of the new, armed arrivals would only get them into further trouble. They had turned into individual, frightened men who knew that their leader had made them go down a path they would never have chosen. Their weapons were taken away and so were they.

25

A day later Jubal Thorne sat in town with Abbey Watt, Starry and Lena. They were in the café rather than the saloon, while someone was minding the bar for the owner of the Wooden Barrel.

'You can thank Lena,' said Starry. 'She came to me and put it that we shouldn't stand by while people were being killed in cold blood. I saw that as a reasonable argument, sure.'

'You took your time getting there,' said Thorne, but his one eye sparkled and a smile tugged at the corners of his mouth.

'We weren't sure of what they were going to do,' said Lena. 'And we didn't want to get into open warfare on the plains. So we waited until they left for the valley and followed. It was all we could do.'

'Stryker will say that I'm a murderer,

that I was hired by Abbey, and that it was all a set-up to rob him of his rights,' said Thorne, a little of the humour fading from his face.

'Then he'll have to decry two witnesses,' said a voice from the doorway. It was Justin Bowers. The young lawyer walked into the room with an air of authority. He wore a good suit and looked about ten years older. He sat down with them.

'I'll stand by all the documents I had written for you and so will my clerk, and remember, there's a third witness to the fact that you visited me that day with Abbey: the owner of this very establishment.'

'So you'll stand up and say that I couldn't have had a motive for killing the old man?'

'In fact you would have had a reason for keeping him with us, if anything,' said Bowers. 'Now his son has a claim on the land and the property.'

'I'll tell you what happened,' said Abbey flatly. 'Tom's property was on the edge of Stryker's. He wanted the old man to sell the land to him, and when he heard about Jubal here, he decided to go up and finish the old man himself.'

'And there's another material fact,' said Bowers. 'He got his connections from the railways to come and offer me a job that would take me away for a long time, so I couldn't back up Thorne's story.'

'Why did you come back?' asked Thorne.

'Because your sheriff asked me to,' said Bowers, 'and because I don't like being set up, and when I saw your telegram I knew that's what had happened.' His mouth quirked a little. 'Besides, there's a certain young lady I had to see.' Thorne remembered Buck had mentioned Amy, the girl in the store, in one of their discussions. He thought her admiration of the young lawyer wasn't as one-sided as he had supposed.

'That's why Stryker moved so fast,'

said Abbey. 'He wanted us dead quickly so that he could finish staking his claim. He knew that Merrill has no children, so he would put a bid in for the eatery and surrounding land straight away, and if any of his men were accused of the murder he would back them up, give them alibis, make sure any possible witnesses were intimidated . . . ' she stopped and nearly broke down. Lena reached over and hugged her friend.

'I made a mistake,' admitted Thorne, 'I thought if there was a confrontation it would happen at the spread I had just bought. I went up there to deal with trouble and make my mark on the place. I didn't know that Stryker had made big plans that he wasn't about to break. Or that he would set the law on me.' He smiled ruefully at the thought.

'Well, you'll be glad to know the sheriff is dropping all charges against you,' said Abbey. 'Although Stryker's lawyers will press like hell to have them reinstated.'

'They can do what they like,' said

Thorne. 'After this is over I'm heading out of here. I'm gifting the land to Tom's son and he can make of it what he wants. Where's Avery?' he added.

'Don't you understand? It's the start of the trail season,' said Abbey. 'There's a thousand head or more of cattle passing through Clearwater right now. The eatery's busier than ever. Why, he's even got Cy and Billy working for him, feeding some mighty hungry riders.'

Thorne did not have to consider the matter for long. Getting back to work was probably the best thing for the big man, given his present circumstances. The long hours in the kitchen and shouting orders at his staff would do him the world of good; it would allow him to retreat away from the horror of what had been done to him.

'Aren't you worried about a revenge attack from the rest of the Cattle Trading Association?' Thorne asked Abbey.

'Are you fooling?' she asked.

'They're finished,' said Starry

'All done,' added Lena.

'You see, since the law has become involved — and if a sheriff and his deputy are attacked in the line of duty there's going to be a lot of explaining to do — the CTA are backing off like nothing else. They want nothing to do with Stryker or his tactics,' said Bowers. 'Even though he made bail, his men are still safely locked up.'

'Then I guess there's nothing more to be said.' Thorne got up. 'I'm moving on right now. I'll be back for the trial.'

'Please stay,' said Abbey, 'I'll always have a place for you.' He looked into her sparkling eyes and realized a truth he had not seen before. Abbey Watt was in love with him. Merrill Avery may once have been her partner, but she was a young woman nearly half his age. She was a good-looking woman with many years ahead of her, while Avery was not in the best of health. She had stayed with him out of duty and nothing else.

'I'll come out with you while you get your things,' she said.

'Sure, I could do with the company,' he said. He wanted to refuse her offer, but she had put him in an awkward situation. They said their goodbyes to the rest. The meeting had been a sort of thank you to the four who had helped save the day, for the masked riders had been Morty — the owner of the café — Lena, Bowers and Starry.

Thorne considered the matter as they made their way back to the spread. It was good to be out in the open with freedom to move and think. Moving on was part of his life; he knew that now, although for a moment he was sorely tempted to stay. Abbey was a fine woman, attractive, hard working, and intelligent. He could do far worse. She respected his silence until they got to the ranch in the hills where he had been planning to make a living. They stood looking at the ramshackle building together after dismounting.

'Guess it was a pipe-dream,' he said.

'Doesn't need to be,' she replied, turning and embracing him. She was warm and pleasant and he did not resist her kisses until she stepped back. 'There's more of that, a lot more.'

'I'm going in to get my things,' he said. 'Come with me.'

'No, I'll stay out here,' she said, disappointment in her voice.

He went inside and fetched what little he had brought with him. He looked around one more time. This was supposed to have been a new start, a new future, but now he couldn't wait to get away. When he walked out, ready to go, she was still standing there. But so was Chas Stryker, and he was holding a gun to her head.

'She's dead,' he said exultantly, 'if you don't get rid of your weapons.'

★　★　★

Throwing down his bag, he took out his Peacemakers and dropped them to the porch of the building where he was still standing, and they landed with a considerable thud. Once more he had underestimated his foe. In his head he had pictured Stryker, whose family had posted a considerable bond for him amounting to 30,000 dollars, going home to sulk and nurse his wounds, not daring to move.

Now he realized what kind of person he was up against: a man who did not care what happened to him anymore as long as he had his revenge.

'Now, move away from them guns,' said Stryker, 'or she still gets it in the head.'

Thorne could hear his spurs jangle, hear his deepening breath and the lowing of cattle in the distance as he stomped down the steps of the porch, so quiet was it out here.

'Now, come with me,' said Stryker, 'I want you both out at Coltsfoot Pass, looking down at the valley.' He did not add that this was the last thing they were going to see, but they both knew what he meant. Thorne was in front as they walked along the uneven ground and out to where the terrain sloped down towards both Brewlins and the valley. The air was still thick with brown dust where the cattle had passed that very morning.

Thorne turned and glared at Abbey with his one good eye.

'Duck,' he said.

Abbey reacted swiftly, she was still gripped by one of Stryker's arms, but it was not a firm grip given that they both needed enough freedom to march and that Stryker was recovering from a wounded shoulder. As she obeyed Thorne's instruction and became a dead weight, her fall was enough to break his grip — he was not a young man and she was a statuesque woman — and she sprawled at his feet. This did not disquiet Stryker in the least; he would simply carry out the final act on her where she lay and he took a second to aim his Colt .45 at her head.

But that second was all that Thorne needed. He had already turned towards the killer when giving his abrupt command, and as he did so his hand had gone to his boot and something flew through the air a bare second later, glinting with deadly beauty in the sunlight.

Stryker looked down in a sort of mild surprise at the knife sticking out of his chest.

'Had to be,' he said, dropping the gun from fingers that could no longer feel. He sank to his knees and pitched forward on to his face. His hat rolled away as he fell, and he was still, the crown of his head silver.

★ ★ ★

Abbey Watt, Merrill Avery and the two boys were there to see him off. He had just eaten his last meal, gratis, at the eatery. He was on the back of Ebony now, his worldly possessions in a saddle-pack behind him. By using almost an entire minute in silence with Abbey, at their last parting they had agreed that staying here was no longer an option for him, no matter how she felt about him.

'You look after this young lady, you

hear?' said Thorne to the two young men. They nodded obediently.

'I wish you could stay,' said Abbey. He smiled for her.

'It's better this way,' he said. 'I wish the circumstances had been easier, but it's been a pleasure knowing you, ma'am, and you too, Merrill.' He rode off then, without looking back. Soon he would be far away on the Oregon Trail and the events in Brewlins would be a distant memory, but a memory nonetheless.

Perhaps he would go back to his old life as a bounty hunter, but he had money enough for his needs and the time might come when he could settle again.

Until then he would ride the trail and try to get rid of the ghosts of the past.